THE COSMIC LAWYER

LAWYER

ARVINDER GREWAL

First paperback edition September 2020

Book design copyright © by Sam Wall (Book cover designer and illustrator) www.samwall.com

ISBN: 9798688118889

IMPRINT: Independently published

As to the reasons why?

This book is dedicated to my son, Rahul. Hopefully one day when he is a bit older, he can read this book and be proud of his daddy. You are my inspiration, son.

During the lockdown when Covid19 was rife, I was struck down with a mild form of the virus. I was completely bedridden, and in isolation, for four days with no TV or phone. During my time tossing and turning, I had various vivid stories going through my head. As a parent, all sorts of negative thoughts run through your mind. I just wanted to write a short sci-fi comic, which my son and I could enjoy together. On the fifth day, when I was feeling a bit better, I remember taking a pen and paper and sitting in the garden for some fresh air. The weather was hot and it was a beautiful, sunny day. As I sat, I thought I could write some notes down and create a character for my son to enjoy. However, five hours later and after 26 pages of A4 paper, I completed what was, essentially, a short story. I couldn't believe it; I couldn't stop writing even when my hand was so tired. I am so glad I did it.

I tried to write the book in such a way that my son could enjoy the story, as well as do further research on any of the topics and facts presented in the book, hopefully you can too.

Acknowledgements - Special thanks to:

I would like to thank my juggernaut of a wife, who thinks I am absolutely crazy, love you loads. My special mom who laid the foundations for me to prosper. My parents, family, the best brothers a person can have and my WhatsApp crew, you know who you are. I would also like to make a special reference to a person who doesn't know how much of an inspiration they have been. Induu, since I can remember as a child, you were an inspiration, a real trailblazer who did not conform to the social norms of the time and pursued careers because you genuinely wanted to do so and not just because of societal pressures. She made me see doors that can be opened at an early age and that you don't have to do things just for the sake of doing things. To everyone, I salute *you and can't thank you enough for the positive impact you have had, directly / indirectly, on my life.*

THE COSMIC LAWYER

Where we at:

Chapter 1 ¬ The Explanation

How does being a loser make you a winner? Cosmo contemplates this strange random thought, as he is dazed and confused, sitting in a cold chair unable to move. Weirdly, there are no cuffs tied to his arms and legs. He immediately tries to look around and establish what he can see or feel. His vision is impaired, but some unnatural force is holding him down. All thoughts, flashbacks and images are running through his mind in sheer panic overdrive. He can hear whispers in front of him, 'This primitive is an embarrassment,' but cannot pinpoint where they are coming from in a dark room, still with blurred vision. Is he dead? Kidnapped? Sleep paralysis? Cosmo has a hard time trying to rationalise his own thought process. He thinks to himself he has never wronged anyone in his life and starts to comb his past for clues.

As Cosmo contemplates his life, his perception of time seems to slow down, panic stricken he starts to compartmentalise his thinking process which is running at breakneck speed. *'How did I get here? What have I done?'* He thinks, frantically trying to search his past for clues. Cosmo takes a deep breath and constructs a mind map thought process starting from the beginning of his life. *'Okay take a deep breath, what's the worst that can happen? Let's start from the beginning'*, Cosmo speaks to himself, trying to relax. Cosmo starts to remember his childhood in flashbacks.

When Cosmo was five years old he spoke to his parents, 'Mommy, Daddy, what will I be when I be bigger?'

'You will be special, our Cossy Wossy.' His mother fawned.

While his dad said, 'You, Cossy will do great things one day; you will have a job, and the biggest house ever!'

'The biggest house, really?' Cosmo said, as a five-year-old child, his mind was blown away.

In the here and now, Cosmo continues to struggle to move, with only his mind and consciousness being free. He searches for more clues in his past narrating to himself in flashbacks. *'Come on hippocampus do your thing! Ever since I can remember, my whole life has been one big struggle. Even before I was born it was a struggle and we have always been poor. My mom was working and dad was sick long-term, but he tried his best around the home to support mom.*

Before he became ill, my dad had a great job as an accountant and was working oversees in India on secondment when he met my mother. My mother, Jasmine, was working in a call centre as a team leader and by chance ended up having a meeting with my dad, Glen. They hit it off from the start, like magnets. My mom was not supposed to be in that meeting, but her boss was ill that day.'

In short flash back sequences in chronological order, Cosmo is putting things together. *'During their time of courting, Jasmine argued with her parents and sisters Mandy and Nisha. Glen always stood by her side, still being respectful to her parents and promised her, they'd make it work, no matter what and with that look and smile that Glen gave, Jasmine knew she'd found her soulmate. After months of arguing with the family, Glen got a call from his bosses to come back to the USA. Jasmine was livid and heartbroken with the news. A few days later, Glen met Jasmine in the flower park where they used to meet in private. Glen was anxiously pacing up and down, nervous as he waited to tell her. Jasmine approached with dread, thinking the worst, but Glen got down on one knee and proposed to her.*

Glen held out a plain diamond ring in front of him. 'I have never felt like this before, I am totally in love with you Hun and I want to grow old with you. I can't guarantee our life will be bliss, let's face it, with your parents' but I can guarantee you, I will love you and be

by your side through bad times and good.'

Glen was an orphan, and his childhood had been spent

moving from one foster home to another with no family

and all he wanted in life was to feel complete. In

Jasmine he found that completeness; a charismatic,

strong-minded, feisty, beautiful woman. She was from a

totally different background, different culture, but he

didn't care, he could not keep his eyes of her.'

This courting story, Jasmine has told Cosmo countless
times. In the present, he concludes nothing related to her
is the reason why he is stuck in a chair. But if he was
kidnapped surely he would have had a mask on his face
and if it is a kidnapping, he is poor financially, with no
assets. He delves further into his past maybe there is
something he can connect or make links with as to why he
is here.

Jasmine surprised, totally taken aback, hugged and kissed

Glen with joyful tears streaming down her face. From

there it had been a rough few months after telling Jasmine's parents and family. Her sisters were happy for her but parents were not impressed. Nevertheless, they managed to get married in a small registry office with her sisters attending. Both of them from the start had a steely determination and an iron will to see it through. This is a characteristic, which Cosmo has unknowingly inherited. *'They both eventually departed India and headed back to the USA to plan the rest of their lives together, excited newlyweds. They eventually bought their first house, where they happily played practical jokes on each other. Glen unsuccessfully tried his best at making traditional Indian curries with disastrous results, burning pans and the kitchen in the process. Jasmine couldn't understand the point of bland fries and both kept bursting into laughter. As they decorated their house, Jasmine was five months pregnant and couldn't stop touching her belly. All of a sudden she looked at Glen, she gasped that she felt unwell and collapsed. She was rushed into hospital. Glen was distraught, worried* and the nurses eventually told him, his wife had had a miscarriage. There was nothing they could do. Glen wept, totally devastated by the news. He found Jasmine who seemed traumatised. The doctor arrived with even more devastating news: she would never be able to have child of her own.

After that, there was a strain on the marriage, causing constant bickering. But every time the argument subsided, Glen would see the amazing woman he had married and would comfort her or would surprise her and make her laugh for a short while.

At work Glen was often asked to come out for a few drinks, but always responded the same: 'My wife needs me'. Glen was there by Jasmine's side through it all, he never left her and nursed her back to health, emotionally and mentally and love between them grew stronger and stronger, overcoming the arguments. Jasmine could have told her parents what she was going through, but thought *it would have been more hassle and stress with more questions, which she couldn't deal with right then.*

As time passed by, both started to enjoy life again and accepted they'd never have children. They went out to restaurants and took vacations, life was back too normal, even if sometimes they pondered 'What if'?'.

In the present, Cosmo concludes it cannot be his parents playing a practical joke. *What is this force holding me down?* He composes himself, he can feel the sweat dripping from his forehead, but there is nothing he can do and continues with his search.

'One day Glen got a phone call from the hospital regarding his wife. Glen rushed there, anxiously abandoning work, and muttering to himself, 'Please don't die. Not anymore worse news, please everything is great at the moment.'

Once there, struggling to breath with all the running, he was greeted by the doctors in Jasmine's ward. They were all smiles and greeting him with congratulations. 'Your wife is five months pregnant; everything is fine.'

Shocked, Glen asked them for a glass of water and to repeat the news again. Glen hugged the doctors and Jasmine explained that she kept the news quiet because she hadn't wanted to get her hopes up again. They were both in stunned disbelief with this great news.

Three months later randomly, when they were doing gardening outside, Jasmine asked Glen, 'What shall we call our baby boy?'

'We're having a boy? Oh my god, that's awesome! Erm let me think...okay, I've got it, how about 'Glen The Second?' Jasmine didn't look impressed and pushed Glen off her. 'No Glen 'The Second then'? Okay, cool... I have no idea, Hun' said Glen. Jasmine punched him on the shoulder as a sign of indirect affection.

A few weeks later, there was a meteor shower all over the news; a red comet splitting up in the atmosphere, a once in a life time event. Jasmine attentively watched the news and shouted at Glen to come over. As Glen ran to her curiously, Jasmine pointed to the floor: her waters had broken. Glen frantically gathered her belongings, muttering to himself 'not to panic'. Hours later, Jasmine has given birth to a healthy baby boy. Both new parents can't stop looking at him in awe.

'What will you call your little bundle of joy?' The nurse asked.

Glen felt perplexed but then Jasmine said, 'We're going to call him Cosmo. He is perfect in every way, our once in a life time event.'

'I love it, Cosmo it is. Welcome to the world, son.' Glen said proudly'

When all three are back at home, Glen does everything he can, works from home and takes care of both of them. Jasmine feels so blessed to have a doting husband and a beautiful baby boy. Her life feels complete and she *couldn't be happier. Both parents look after Cosmo, playing with him, taking him to parks, shopping and on holidays. Jasmine's parents also stopped fighting with her and are in regular communication'*

In the here and now, Cosmo is still struggling to move out of his chair but the room seems to be lighter now. He is less panicked, he definitely isn't 'adopted' then, questioning himself. Being kidnapped by parents who are serial killers or something; it was a weird sense of humour coming out from Cosmo. *'Keep looking, must stay focused'*, he thinks to himself.

'A few years later, I remember my mom telling me when I was around five, dad was told he had stage two lung cancer during a routine health check. Mom was devastated by the news, but stayed strong for dad, provided the support he needed to stop him from breaking down and through it all helped him to recover. The medication and therapies left dad in a lot of pain. The firm dad worked for, stopped paying halfway through

his medical treatments because of the clause in the small print, in his work contract. This would define and reshape dad's thinking for the rest of his life. Dad thought about fighting his case but with his health so fragile, he just couldn't do it. Mom and dad eventually decided to sell their home to pay for his treatment and move into a small two-bedroom apartment. My mom managed to get a job as a secretary at a top firm of lawyers. Her boss was a complete moron. But mom put up with Sheila so they could pay the bills. Over the years, one thing that never fell apart was their love and admiration for each other which grew stronger each day'.

In the present, Cosmo still sitting in his ice cold chair reflects and concludes his parents are one hundred percent clean, they have not wronged anyone either with potential enemies. They are not the reason he is stuck in a chair.

'*Parents done, now me.*' Cosmo narrates to himself, with an affectionate tear in his eye admiring what his parents went through.

'*Ever since I can remember, I have been awesome, special, and spectacular at being a complete loser. In school, I was always a loser; I just never really fitted in. I was picked on, called names. I was, to be honest, an odd ball, maybe even socially inept. My teacher diagnosed me as having mild 'Autism Spectrum Disorder, saying I was really bright, full of potential'. It was never officially registered because my hot-headed mother refused to believe it, thinking I was perfect in every way and just didn't understand it. I would create all these barriers and walls in my mind, being hesitant with everything like making friends and second guessing myself on tests. I would find my solace in reading books of all kinds, from super hero comics, studying animals and how the world works to reading about the universe and listening to all types of music to help me focus. I would make friends* then put my foot in it somehow, and boom, friendship finished and the cycle kept repeating. When other kids were invited to parties, I couldn't go because my dad was too ill and we couldn't afford it'

'At high school I was an even bigger loser. I had relationships, but it was more for pranks or as a pity charity case. I wasn't the most outspoken in class, or confident or athletic. I suppose I could have got fit in high school to impress the girls, but I just couldn't be bothered to try at that point, as the result would be the same as it always had been. Most of my time was spent looking after my dad, while everyone else would go to the coast and party. I couldn't project the confident image I had of myself in my mind into reality. It was like there were two sides to me a reflection in the mirror, one dying to get out but I just couldn't do it. Most of the time I kept to myself. I had chances to go out but when the time would come, I had to look after my father or I would be too hesitant and overthink it.'

'But, really, I didn't mind this because growing up, my dad was the best. We couldn't afford to do much, but my dad got me into soccer. At school, we would play and no matter how ill my dad was, he would always come and see me play. 'Keep challenging, climbing Cosmo. Serenity is around the corner.' My dad always said with pride. The only time I didn't feel like a loser, was when I scored the winning goal in one match. I had that feeling of pure 'serenity'; I knew what my dad meant. After analysing all the teams in the world, we both chose to support Wolverhampton Wanderer in the English Second Division, mainly because as a kid I loved wolves. I loved the whole notion of a pack mentality. In my family too, we were a pack, a close-knit family, all three of us. From an early age my dad and I would watch all Wolves' matches on TV. Every time we would win matches in school, we would get special badges as a reward. I would always etch a W on my badges to replicate the team emblem.

I remember one time when I was ten; I got so frustrated with my parents for not letting us attend the celebrations after school matches. My parents would always say we couldn't afford it. One time in particular, I got so mad I screamed at my parents, 'I hate being so poor.' In response my mum calmly took my hand and next minute we were on a bus to a small town. We ended up in a soup kitchen helping the homeless. There my mum explained that though we were poor, there were people a lot, lot worse off. My mind was blown away. My mom explained that people here had jobs and were doing really well, but that when businesses close for good, it can have dire consequences on people's lives. She had taken me there because her law firm were the ones who closed down the factories because of unpaid rents. This was my first ever experience of economics 101 supply and demand and I learnt to be grateful for the things we had after that. We were greeted by one of the volunteers and her daughter, who was roughly the same age as me. The young daughter gave me a 'take pride' badge and told me *her name was Sofia. I shyly told her my name was Cosmo. She made that face that everyone makes of confusion at hearing my name and in return I gave her one of my W badges. We played all through the afternoon together that day and shared our first kiss together, pure serenity. Back at home sometimes my dad had good days, some days he was in constant pain, so I quit my soccer team. It was the least I could do. The one thing I could not bear, was seeing my dad in pain. I could see how much it helped him, for a short time, forget the pain circulating around his chest. I would come home after school and dad and I would watch wrestling or magic shows and guess how the magic was done. We would often discuss life, economic issues, sometimes life's not fair and how, if we had all the money in world how could we use it, what would we buy or would we help people?'*

'Dad told me, 'Son, always have back up plans to back up plans.'.

This was his mantra after everything that had happened and he only wanted me to be careful about the choices I made. Mom would secretly borrow law books from the office and make me read them, like it was a religion to her. She would see all these successful lawyers and wanted the same for me so I would not have to worry about finances.

'Who can blame her? One minute everything is great, next minute your life can take a freefall. At college and law school, I scraped through the various law and bar exams. I was juggling looking after my dad and a part-time job, washing dishes at a local Korean restaurant with an angry owner. Then I was a qualified freshman lawyer, my life would be great from then on. I felt top of the world; both my parents were at graduation looking so proud.'

In the present, Cosmo thinks it cannot be someone from his childhood as most of the time he kept to himself. *So why am I here?* He starts to search nearer to the present after the graduation, thinking of anything, trying to search for clues. Meanwhile, he can start to see clear shadows in the room; his vision is coming back, his movement is still restricted.

'After graduation, a few months later, I was constantly writing different job application forms, attending interview after interview, getting rejection after rejection. 'Not clever enough', 'not fitting the profile', 'losing out to better, superior, chiselled-chin candidates'. I was distraught after every rejection and seeing other candidates I went to college with, all getting the jobs I was applying for, it was soul destroying.'

'I did what any self-respecting person would do. I got a job as a janitor in a law firm and pretended I was working as a lawyer to my parents. The look of disappointment would have been too much for me to bear.'

In the present, Cosmo is still held in a chair and still cannot move his body. When suddenly he sees at the corner of his eye something entering his mouth, he is powerless to stop it, full of dread and horror. The texture of this moving furry thing circulating in his mouth, tastes like a 'rum' drink. He thinks he will puke up but he doesn't, he cannot feel the furry thing at all. This triggers another flashback which leads to the present here and now.

Years passed and my parents did not question anything. One day, my mom was on the phone to her mom back in India.

On speaker phone, 'Happy Diwali everyone! How is Glen doing and how is Cosmo doing? Is Cosmo a manager yet? I am worried who is going to marry him? Jasmine, what are you doing about this? You know Mandy and Nisha's children are doctors, accountants and CEOs now. Married with children, settled down, they are all extremely successful.' Grandma says in a patronising manner.

'Happy Diwali to you to. That's great, Mother, will you be coming here to celebrate Christmas?' Glen can be seen in the background miming and waving "'no, no, no way'".

'Glen and Cosmo are fine, doing really well. Oh, oh, someone's at the door, I have to go. I will ring you soon regarding festivities, Mother. Bye.' My mother looked frustrated.

Dad spoke from behind her. 'Did you just farzee your mom again?'

Mother laughed. Farzee is a made up word both Glen and Jasmine use in times of crises or if they are doing something silly and want to vent their frustration.

'She is so annoying sometimes. Everyone is amazing, except us and she always has to rub our noses in it!' mother replied, as she stamped her feet on the ground.

'Hun, you're having a farzee. Relax, take a deep breath. Your mum has been doing this for, what, twenty, thirty years now? Relax.' Dad said calmly.

'I walked out of the apartment saying goodbye to my parents with a piece of toast in my mouth. I was thirty years old, in a dead-end job, watching as other workers who started off as janitors slowly moved out and moved up in the career ladder. How was this possible? I had all the credentials, trying my best. Was it just bad luck? I kept trying so hard for a break. It gets to you after a while, drinking takes over, going to work drunk and then one day you get fired for drinking excessively at work which happened to be on the same day as my grandma rang to brag about her other successful grandchildren.'

'I was feeling bitter about the way my life had worked out so far: no girlfriend, no friends, no real job. I saw people that were in my class who were in successful careers, in relationships, driving flashy cars, basically everything I wished I could have and be. I would think to myself, 'How did life become so crap?'. I purchased a bottle of rum from the local shop and sat on a park bench that evening. I just couldn't face going home to tell my parents I'd been fired, after finding out today how well my family is doing in India. Thanks grandma, much appreciated. The looks of disappointment would be too much too bear after everything my parents have been through. I sat there drinking my rum straight from the bottle and passed out on the bench.'

In the here and now Cosmo thinks it's obvious, '*I am still drunk and this is a hallucination it has to be, what else could it be? I'm a good person I don't deserve this. Is it mistaken identity? I have nothing, I'm nothing, a nobody.*'

Chapter 2 ¬ Welcome to Blends

In the present, Cosmo now remembers. *'So I lay on the park bench passed out until late evening when I was awoken. I can remember vaguely a small glow that appeared around and behind me with four small green dots scanning my whole body. With what seemed to be bright yellow fish swimming around me, rapidly like a tornado. It must have transported me to this room. Abducted by aliens? Don't be silly Cosmo! So this was not a dream, I wasn't just hallucinating? Surely this is not a weird government experiment or a figment of my imagination? So this all happened?'* Cosmo concludes.

Still incapacitated, Cosmo's vision has cleared up. He looks everywhere in the room in all directions, where his eyes can gaze upon. To his surprise, around him lies what can only be described as a large meeting room, a partially viewed table in front of him, with icons, pictures, wallpaper taken from the images of his bedroom. The ceiling above, is a bright blue sky with birds flying and beautiful clouds hovering; it looks so real, there is a glitch in the sky which indicates to Cosmo that it is an artificial construct of some kind. The floor beneath him is laid out like green grass which smells freshly cut like from Cosmo's childhood park, playing soccer. There is memorabilia of famous models from the past to the present. There are pictures of sporting icons from boxing to wrestling, well-known magicians and one of Cosmo's soccer club, Wolves. This room is basically Cosmo's personality. As Cosmo is slumped on a spacious silver chair he starts to come around trying to figure out the reasons why he is here, still being held by an unknown force This force once again is making his mouth open wide, slowly.

All of a sudden, slowly, another slimy blue and purple, shiny worm enters Cosmos mouth via a floating tube device as Cosmo looks horrified, with nothing but his eyes moving frantically around. Cosmo passes out again, at the same time all his senses are exploding all at once in his mind and body. The tension on his body feels less restricted from the shaking. Cosmos head feels like it is somewhat experiencing 'exploding head syndrome', the sounds in his mind akin to crashing waves which seem to get louder and louder, to the point where Cosmo wakes up.

Cosmo's twenty-twenty vision starts to come around, he has a thumping headache, he starts to hear again all sorts of voices ridiculing him loud and clear. There is no taste or any evidence left in his mouth, that he has just swallowed a disgusting looking worm.

'That thing is so disgusting.'

'It's cerebral cortex is so small with so few neurons!'

'It smells funny.'

'Need to make this quick.'

'I feel nauseous looking at him, I hope we don't catch anything.'

'We just need his permission, then we are done.'

'You're right, he does smell weird.'

'Send in Alluca.'

At first Cosmo is dreading who Alluca is, his first thought, thinking some sort of government agent, who is going to torture him. Secondly why do they need his permission? He thinks to himself surprisingly. His mouth is now unrestrained and can actually speak, coughing, making adult crying noises, still in somewhat of a daze,

'Please, please stop, leave me alone, I haven't done anything to anybody. You have got the wrong guy, a mistaken identity. Please let me go, I am begging. Please look at my driver's licence, it's in my pocket. I don't want to die, I have rights!' A thousand random images, flashbacks racing through Cosmo's head, heart beating faster, the feeling of anticipation is unbearable.

Just then a mix of jazz and light beat tunes start playing like in an elevator, in the room around him. For a few moments, this eases Cosmo's anxiety and stress levels.

'This is going to be effortless, pathetic species.' Cosmo hears again a voice in the background.

After a few moments, the elevator tunes stop. There is another weird sound almost like a forklift truck picking up a heavy pallet. Cosmo is staring at where the sound is coming from. Suddenly a young looking female figure approaches Cosmo and emerges out from the green mist which has come on, in front of him. This light green, steamy mist, waterfall is continuously flowing towards the ground, behind her, as she walks to the chair in front of him. She sits down slowly in a professional intimidating manner. In front of her is an old mahogany table, sat on the other side facing her directly is Cosmo. Cosmo's sheer panic mode has subsided a little, whilst totally being gobsmacked.

'This is Alluca?' He is fascinated and in a trance by her beautiful presence at the same time shaking his head in disbelief.

Cosmo emphatically speaks to himself in his mind. '*Wow, just wow, this is Alluca? What can I say about Alluca? She is absolutely stunning. Tall, slim with wavy brown hair, clear, tanned skin and beautiful green eyes. Her arms are toned and her body encased in a classy business outfit. She looks like a mixture of all the pictures of models on my bedroom wall. She could easily make a guy skip a heartbeat, making him breathless and speechless. Yes, I'm talking about myself. Why am I talking to myself in this way? I sound a little creepy.*' Cosmo is trying to justify it to himself.

Alluca looks directly at Cosmo, who is now fully aware of his surroundings, fully conscious and free of the force that had held him on the chair. Even though Cosmo can fully move and is fidgeting, he doesn't want to get up and run, mainly because of Alluca's presence. Alluca starts talking in a French-American accent, but all Cosmo hears is a muffled sound and added to the fact how stunning this person is sat in front of him, he is speechless.

'I'm really sorry can you repeat what you said? I promise I will try to focus and pay attention,' Cosmo says fearfully.

Alluca then pauses, looks around the room, then directly at Cosmo, she calmly speaks.

'Alright, let me repeat myself, firstly sorry you sat there longer than anticipated, incapacitated. It takes longer for your primitive body to adjust compared to other species we meet. It's for your own safety the bioganatizer was used to restrict your movement which can cause disorientation in the process, for this I humbly apologise.' She further explains, looking at Cosmo who has a confused look by squinting his eyes.

'The bioganatizer is like a magnet but rather pushing and pulling iron materials, the bioganatizer can pull bio organisms, any species and hold them down accordingly in every capacity possible, to suit what purpose it is intended for. In your case to restrict your movement from doing self-harm and help you adjust expeditiously.' Alluca looks at Cosmo, who seems a little less confused and can see him process this information.

'Secondly, my name is Alluca and welcome to Blends.' She gestures as to say this is the room they are both sat in. 'I hope you been treated fairly under our guidance of your CX321 rights. The room is an artificial construct that has been adjusted, to suit and meet your wellbeing needs. This room is not a virtual reality or a place of construct in your mind, but is real and what you are experiencing is genuinely truthful. Most importantly, listen carefully,' Alluca then speaks in a firm authoritative manner. 'This is a meeting of planetary contract negotiations. Your input is vital to have a successful and positive outcome from this meeting. Are you with me so far?' Cosmo still gobsmacked, nods his head hesitantly.

She points to herself, 'We, Zargboyans, are in your primitive species form, to make you feel as comfortable as possible and so that no miscommunication takes place. We are using Blends illusion sensors to do this and have been only used for this intended meeting. Comply with us and it will be very short and you can get back home to do what you were doing.'

Alluca then smiles at Cosmo. She can see that Cosmo is fully aware and making reasonable communication. She shows her standard issue business card to Cosmo and places it on the table in front of him. It displays 'Alluca Manzcilla, Intergalactic Lawyer, KillaRhinepor Corporation. There is a logo, which looks like '¬' on the top right of her business card.

Cosmo picks up her business card, which has a clear shine on it now. The feeling of the material paper, changes, and he gets a slight shock all over his body. The business card flies out of his hand and onto the table again near

Alluca. Cosmo is shocked and taken back, 'Is this some sort of magic trick, magnets?' Cosmo speaks all flustered.

Alluca smiles, 'No, no magic trick, just my standard business card which is linked to me personally'.

She shrugs and looks at Cosmo with contempt like a baby playing with a sophisticated phone. 'Fascinating, ninety-nine point nine percent of all organisms to have lived on your planet are extinct, and yet here you remain, as the dominant species.' Alluca quietly mutters to herself consciously looking around the room, whilst Cosmo is still distracted and intrigued by the business card.

'Wow, not seen a business card do that before.' Cosmo speaks.

'Oh you will be surprised. Shall we continue?' Alluca asks.

'Sure, I guess,' Cosmo nodding his head.

'Let's continue with the formal proceedings then,' Alluca says in calm and authoritative manner and raises both her arms.

At that very moment Alluca's entourage appears from the glowing green mist waterfall behind her on the back wall. There are ten human looking species altogether, half male, half female, and all amazing-looking model lawyers. Everyone has something to say and a piece of information to divulge during the meeting. Cosmo looks at them all, he seems to be intimidated by these models who look to be perfect in every way possible. Heightening an inferiority complex he has had all his life.

At this point Cosmo is stunned and does not know how to react, or what to feel or say. He is pinching himself to make sure he is conscious and that the people he is looking at are actually real. His anxiety and panic stress has been alleviated by the presence of Alluca. He finds it hard to keep his eyes off her, as for the first time, he has the undivided attention of a beautiful stunning female sat before him.

The 'Model Lawyers' are all sat down looking directly at Cosmo, like he is an insignificant insect that is in their way. A few of them can be seen whispering to each other and looking at their business cards nodding in agreement. Alluca is sat in the middle of them, making sure all the lawyers are in place and ready to proceed, she gestures to one of them to start with the proceedings.

Chapter 3 ¬ The Models

Male model lawyer one pipes up and starts the proceedings. He is mixed race with shaved hair, just like a fine specimen of a man who should be on an aftershave commercial. *'Those white teeth...how is it even possible to be that perfect?'* Cosmo thinks to himself.

'First of all, can you hear clearly and can you understand me speaking?' He asks. It reminded Cosmo of how his mom used to speak to him when he was five.

Cosmo nods his head, 'I can hear you loud and clear, though my head feels weird and I have a ringing in my ear.' Cosmo says in a nervous, insecure manner.

'Yes your head hurts because you are acclimatising out here on Planet 4X322 also known as Neptune in your native language. Your hearing will be fine in exactly five seconds as a result from you swallowing the earbime worms. Can I get you a glass of water, coffee? Maybe a cookie, biscuit?' Model One looks at his other colleagues with a smirk. Cosmo is starting to get agitated.

'Please, please, I have done nothing wrong,' He says. Model One seems shocked at Cosmo's pitiable condition.

'Can you tell me what the hell is going on? Am I still passed out? Have I been kidnapped, is this a government experiment? Is this a dream, or even a sick joke, prank? Tell me what's going on please! What you're saying is ridiculous and makes no sense.'

'No, you are fully conscious Mr Griffin, please remain calm. No need to panic, just breath slowly and concentrate on my voice, focus on me. Cosmo Griffin, that is your name?' Alluca replies as she shows holographic images from her business card of the solar system for Cosmo to view and various pictures of Cosmo's past. Cosmo is astonished at the technology, like something you would see on TV about the future.

'Yes, it is. How do you know my name, what is all of this, you're showing me? I look around and it's my bedroom.' Cosmo looks inquisitively.

'We know everything about you: what you eat, your history with education and work, lawyer credentials, past relationships, your bowel movements...shall I carry on?' Alluca says in a confident manner.

'Erm no, hold on my bowel movements.' Cosmo squinting his eyes whilst shaking his head.

'Two times a day, pretty efficient.' Alluca smiles. 'Look, every living planet that is developed has lawyers in some capacity. On your planet we chose you. Under the universal 4.23.6 clause, every living planet must be represented by a credible lawyer to initiate proceedings regarding the host planet. In other words, you, Mr Cosmo Griffin, are representing your planet and we chose you to conduct these contractual negotiations on your planet's behalf.' Alluca says again in firm voice.

Cosmo is totally stunned, it was not the response he was expecting, blowing his cheeks, sitting back, looking around the room, point the finger at himself miming, 'Me, me.' Cosmo then responds in a delayed reaction after a quick shake of his head.

'Hold on! Wait, what? Represent in terms of what? Wow. Wow, this is crazy, now I know I am definitely dreaming.' Cosmo emits a nervous insecure laugh.

Female model lawyer two, a stunning redhead with piercing blue eyes, who should be on a shampoo commercial, pipes up. 'You are definitely not dreaming and there is a strict criteria, which we have to follow and make no mistake. You were chosen with the upmost integrity.' She looks at the other model lawyers, again with that same smirk. 'Your planet is in need of...remodelling, let's say. Your planet CX321 or Earth as you call it, it never belonged to your species and belongs to the KillaRhinepor Corporation. We are the representative lawyers for the KillaRhinepor Corporation.'

'Killer Rhino? What kind of stupid name is that for a corporation? A corporation that owns planet Earth? That is nuts!' Cosmo mutters to himself.

'Mr Griffin, please pay attention.' says Male model lawyer three, who is of eastern Asian background, with skull-crushing muscles peeking out from his shirt. 'This is what we propose. We are willing to let your species stay the dominant species on your planet and let the sub-species on your preoccupied land, stay as it is. In return, all we want is access to your unoccupied land, water and moon facilities. We can make the whole process as swift as possible and no species within your planet will be hurt in the process.' Cosmo is baffled and shocked at the same time. He nervously responds.

'Right, when you say access to water, land and moon facilities, what the hell are you talking about?'

Model Three looks confused and perplexed with Cosmo asking basic questions to which he has already answered in a clear calm manner. He looks at the other model lawyers with his arms in the air as if to ask, did he just not explain this to the primitive?

Female model lawyer four, who is a stunning blonde and looks like one of the model pictures on the wall replies, 'Hell, we're not exactly sure what that means.'

She pauses for a few seconds whilst looking at her own business card and responds, 'We will drain 75% of your planet's water, take 30% land minerals from your planet and moon and transfer it to our resources chamber. It will then be distributed out to other subsidiary sector corporations to distribute even further to other planets. Everything done within twenty-four hours of peace and comfort. It's just business, I'm sure you can appreciate that? Besides your species is incapable of appreciating the resources that your planet holds. Leave it to us, we will look after it.' She squints her eyes whilst she shrugs almost like a fake smile.

Cosmo raises his eyebrows, as thinking that what they are asking is pure fantasy and they haven't even shown any empathy towards the animals on his planet or other life forms. Cosmo is a bit more relaxed and is more sure of himself now, as he is getting to grips with the situation presented in front of him. For some reason, he finds it easier to be communicating with aliens rather than his own kind as he questions himself.

'Well, this seems fair,' Cosmo says sarcastically. He pauses for a few moments, 'Are you nuttttts? You are out of your mind. There are loads of species on land and sea not to mention bacteria etc. You will kill all of that just to put it into a jumped up stock cupboard? What happened to no species will be hurt? Can no one see the irony here? Not to mention the whole disruption to our eco and weather systems, the long term impact on my planet.'

The model lawyers are taken back, like a child having a tantrum.

'That's right, you can't hurt species when consciously they don't feel anything or remember it,' Shrugs Model

Four. 'Besides, when we take the land and water, we will not touch the species, but vaporise them and make sure your ecosystem can still survive and thrive with twenty-five percent water left and replace, top up the rest with a saline solution; a win-win situation, but, importantly, your species survives. If you are really upset, we can create a large tanker for all the species who have been displaced and have no vaporising as an option, but we will require 80% of your water to cover costs. Or we have a cheaper alternative option: we can plant and place more of the oldest species on your planet, the sponges in your oceans, which all basic life on your planet has derived from. It will take approximately 300 million years initially for normalities to arise again, evolution takes forever it seems on your planet.' Another smirk as he is doing some calculations on his business card.

Cosmo is totally bewildered by the sheer arrogance of demands and shakes his head, implying no chance of this happening. How can that be a reasonable demand?

'Can you stop making these ridiculous smirks? This is serious! You are about to destroy my planet. Leaving my species alive, destroy the rest and all you can say is, we will make sure it is less painful, super easy, barely an inconvenience. YOU GUYS ARE INSANE! And you want me to represent my planet and give you the go ahead not to mention this is species genocide, no matter how small or large, is that correct? As corporate lawyers, you can live with this?'

Male model lawyer five, who is of Spanish origin, with thick black hair, a lean build and with an accent even Cosmo's mom would appreciate, interjects and tries to calm Cosmo down by his hand gestures. 'Well, you are a qualified lawyer please start negotiating your terms. This is a great contract and sees your species not only surviving, but thriving. Look, we need to hurry this up. Can you please sign on the dotted line? You can get back home and continue enjoying your sleep. Come on you know in your heart this is true. We are even willing to give you free saline solution to top up your planet's water levels, granted it will not be the same, but my colleagues have given you numerous options. Come on work with me, I am your friend, let's be reasonable about this.' Male model five points to his chest towards the direction of his heart, trying to win Cosmo over.

'Oh, cool yeah, sorry to inconvenience you...Now let me think...Absolutely not! And no schmoozing will change that fact!' Cosmo replies with a little more confidence now, thinking maybe this is his once in a life time event as Cosmo's mom said when he was born, things happen for a reason and he should do something about this?

At this point in the meeting, Cosmo cannot believe how brazen and annoyed these model lawyers are, at the thought of someone questioning them. When Cosmo calms down he takes a deep breath and with clarity of thought, wonders to see the contract fully and remembers his law training and dad religiously telling him 'Always read the small print son,' when he was younger.

'Hold up, can I actually see this planetary contract?' Asks Cosmo. Female model lawyer six of petite build and east Asian background, again, beautiful: jet black hair, plump pink lips. 'Oh, this is what they call sarcasm,' She says giggling. 'Funny, I thought it would be a lot funnier. Here is the contract we propose Mr Griffin, please let me know if you need any assistance. There are some complicated words in the contract, if you refer section 1 and 2, that is all you need to know. I am here for you!' She then giggles and winks at Cosmo.

Cosmo starts to blush and momentarily is distracted. The contract is a one hundred page stacked A4 document. Cosmo grabs the contract and goes straight to the small print which is at the back, looking specifically at the different clauses. Cosmo remembers his dad speaking with the medical insurance provider when he was a kid. They asked, 'What, you didn't read the small print? We are not responsible for your incompetence.' Cosmo remembers the impact this had on his family, so he asks the models for a 'pen and paper.' Model lawyer six is stunned and looks at Alluca, she is confused with his request.

Alluca looks at her business card, suddenly a female Artificial Intelligent robot appears out from Alluca's business card and onto to the floor in solid state form. About three foot in length, the robot has three parts: her face, her body and her legs, which is more like a hover board. The hair protruding from her head are like two arms a bit like fibre optics, as well as the two normal robotic arms on her body. She has LU234C00021 written on her chest and is completely yellow, except her face which is pink with purple digital eyes and mouth. Cosmo has to rub his eyes and look again as he has never seen a sophisticated robot like this before, which validates his scepticism. *Are these real aliens at all? They certainly indeed are.* Thinking in his head.

'Here you go, Mr Griffin, your standard pen and paper, as requested.' The AI acts very professional, with natural quick movement. All the models are looking perplexed at

Cosmo's audacity, including Alluca who is taken back. Cosmo is making notes, scribbling on his piece of paper frantically with various arrows and diagrams, pointing to the small print, looking through it with precision. Sweat is coming from his hands and onto the paper, desperate to make his case points water tight. He notices the first clause which states that all business must be allocated in the allotted time period, which is thirty minutes. Cosmo thinks of stalling, as it has already been twenty minutes by his reckoning. Clause 2.36 states that all species of the host planet must not be harmed directly as a consequence of direct actions imposed on them. Cosmo thinks to himself, *If this is a real corporation, like any other, this one, will probably care about avoiding the negative press.* Clause 2.42 says species must not be affected by the new ecosystem.

Meanwhile, some of the lawyers are holding their noses from the weird smell emitting from Cosmo generated by his sweat. Zargboyans have an acute smell function. Smell to Zargboyans is like DNA; everyone is unique. For Zargboyans and their culture, smell forms an integral part, from courting, to social and professional life, it is synonymous with looks and the character of individuals they interact with.

Female model lawyer seven, who is clasping her nose, looks Scandinavian in origin, tall with shiny, blonde hair, asks male model lawyer eight,

'What is he doing? This is outrageous, is he just wasting our time?'

'I have no idea, it seems like he is making some notes,' replies male model eight with a South African accent as he shrugs his shoulders. 'Can we hurry this up? Time is of the essence, if you need a hand, I can explain it for you!'

'Oh really, time is of the essence you say. How come? I mean, there are over a billion species on my planet that depend on my decision,' Cosmo, more self-assertive, replies.

Female model lawyer nine, who looks bizarrely like a younger version of Cosmo's mother, chimes in.

'Look, we have other planets to discuss business with and need to get this done. We have prepared all documents in your native language to make this process as comfortable as possible for you, if you need my help Cossy, I am right here. You know that picture to the side of you, your parents would be so proud of you. It seems like all three of you had a good time that day. Come on, sign the contract, do it for your special and loving parents.' She tries to win Cosmo over with empathy and affection. She tilts her head and smiles at Cosmo, just like his mom does.

Even though each lawyer has something to say, when and why they say it, seems to be interlinked with Cosmo's past history and relationships. It is like they are trying to exploit Cosmo's weaknesses and insecurities via different emotions of Cosmo's fragility, emitting from these lawyers to get a quick outcome. Cosmo can see through this charade and remains focused on his note making and key research. The model lawyers are increasingly getting annoyed, with all their psychological warfare tactics failing to persuade Cosmo to sign the contract. Their subtle manipulation of intimidating Cosmo has also failed to have the desired effect, for a quick outcome.

Model lawyer seven mutters under her breath, 'I really need to get home and watch the final of 'Zargboyan's True Destiny.'' The other models start looking at their business cards and pointing.

'Exactly, the finale guys,' Model Seven says as she gestures with her arms, 'So please hurry up, Mr Griffin,' in a firm voice.

Meanwhile, Alluca is speaking to her AI who is directly behind her and interjects, 'Mr Griffin, good news, we are willing to waiver the five percent water needed to compensate for all species displaced and are happily able to do this option for free. Obviously we can't give you incentives or technology enhancements for your planet to thrive on. As this violates all protocols and is seen as a form of bribery, where only the few benefit rather than the whole planet. Importantly, we are guaranteeing no species small or big will be harmed period. What do you say, Mr Griffin?'

For the first time since being there, Cosmo thinks he has found a chink in the armour of the lawyers and as alien as they might be, they actually might not be that different from humans after all.

'I'm still thinking.' Cosmo replies, totally focused and thinks he is onto something.

'You wouldn't be tricking us into delaying over the allotted thirty minutes of negotiations so it will become null and void, are you?' Alluca asks.

All the models make a face palm and some mutter, 'So amateurish. Really. Oh please, so layman. Like taking Zargboyan candy from a Gauwladyke.'

'Oh please, have some self-respect,' Alluca shouts in a firm voice. 'Clause 2.04:1 negotiations can be extended indefinitely if decisions have failed to reach a conclusion, let me save you the time.'

Cosmo is half-listening to their conversation while still going through the small print. Clause 4.36 states that once a lawyer has been chosen to represent the host planet, this cannot be changed until the lawyer gives permission to do so. To buy himself more time and probe a bit more he asks,

'So guys, tell me about your Zargboyan drama, the finale, it sounds really interesting.' Cosmo says, whilst scribbling diagrams on his piece of paper.

'Oh the reality show? Unlike on your planet the alpha species is you, homo sapiens. However, on our planet we like to think we, Zargboyans are the true alphas. Although this is not the case, as there are plenty of other sub species who would also call themselves alpha species with generally the same intellect as ours. Imagine a planet with different species co-habiting in harmony, quite extraordinary. Going back to the reality show, after many rounds a Zargboyan child has been chosen from million other contestants from all different species on our planet to represent us in the finals. The child finalist will be discarded, thrown to the scrap heap, or even worse, will bring shame to the family, if the child doesn't perform or close his first contract negotiation. It is the number one live show broadcasted everywhere.' Explained Model Seven before being rudely interrupted by Model Five in excitement.

'But if the child wins, they will have a lifetime contract with the Nurozeip Corporation and a great career in front of them, fast tracked to stardom with Alluca giving the award. Alluca, you're an amazing judge on the show by the way. This validates us, Zargboyans, that we are the superior intellectuals over the other sub species on our planet.' The rest of the models are excited about this show coming to a conclusion and seem weirdly emotionally invested.

'Please everyone, be quiet, what is wrong with you all? So, do we have a deal?' Alluca asks Cosmo, whilst being annoyed at the rest of the lawyers.

Cosmo then takes a deep breath, 'Well, everything seems to be in order on your part, you have been very accommodating and hospitality has been top notch.' With a gleeful mordacity in his voice, Cosmo is looking more and more confident, with both hands behind his head whilst leaning back.

'I'm glad you came to your sense. Let's wrap this up.' Alluca says with a relief, which seems to sweep through all the models who can't wait to get back.

'Erm, I just have a few questions and yeah, no I'm not signing Jack.' Cosmo says with his arms folded and for the very first time looking quite confident and assured with himself.

'Who is Jack?' Asked quintessential Brit, male model lawyer ten. 'Does he not understand the language? Maybe it is too advanced for this primitive; we need to pick another lawyer capable to see sense and make the right decision.'

'Ohhhhh, let me guess that's sarcasm again, right?' Says Model Three looking at the other models.

Alluca looks really frustrated and squints her eyes towards Cosmo.

'Everyone be quiet!' She turns aggressively to Cosmo. 'Sign it. This is a great deal; other planets do not even get the option. We have protected every species on your planet albeit in a reduced capacity. We have given you options, the contract is water tight.'

It had become apparent to Cosmo through the meeting, that these model lawyers look like various people from his past, who he found intimidating and made him feel inadequate. They were playing psychological warfare on him throughout the contract negotiations, subtly with every trick in the book. Seeing through this gives Cosmo the impetus to stand up for himself. Cosmo has a flashback to when he and his dad used to watch programmes about the art of deal making, where they would make the person think they won and at the last minute pull the rug out from underneath them, dashing any hope of negotiation success, frustrating the individual emotionally and get them to make mistakes. He knows time is of the essence for these lawyers, whether it is to see their finale of the TV show or other meetings to attend. Somehow could he exploit this as he scribbles some last minute notes?

Cosmos's dad would often tell him his crackpot theories he'd concocted after spending so much time at home and to help Cosmo process information logically. One particular theory that stuck with Cosmo was his dad's ER's theory; to be successful, people are categorised into four principled topics.

'Cosmo, there are four types of people in this world: wishers, thinkers, deciders and doers. If you pigeon-hole yourself into one of these categories, you will never succeed in life. But use them in tandem, the possibilities are endless. To wish something, you need a dream, an idea, then you start to think strategically. You decide what options you have and go and do it, make it happen, no more barriers in the mind. I call this theory the ER's theory, the evolution, revolution theory of changing the mindset.' Cosmo's dad would often help him process information, because he was on the spectrum, by inventing new theories which would help Cosmo going forward in life.

There is an element of truth in this theory that felt important to Cosmo in this particular moment. Cosmo now felt a steely determination. He was going to confront his past demons with wit and experience, head on. No longer was he going to feel like a loser and accept it as just bad luck or feel intimidated by successful looking people. He was done feeling sorry for himself. The thought of disappointing his own parents forever was suddenly enough motivation, and for the first time in his life, he was not going to be a push over or be ridiculed.

What is the worst that could happen? They'd kill him or torture him, but at least he would have done the right thing and finally make his parents proud, thirty years too late, maybe? Cosmo looks at his notes, making last minute preparations. This is it, the moment that will define his life, Cosmo hopes. Accountability is key, he has a strategy in mind. All he has to do, is present and put his main points across. He looks and thinks about his options; whether to go direct or open with a story to convey his message the most effective way. He has done all he can in the short amount of time, will it be enough he asks himself once more.

Chapter 4 ¬ This Is Crazy

Cosmo is looking at his notes, he stands up. He thinks about his strategy, he has already evoked an emotional reaction from these models and has an idea of how to utilise this. He closes his eyes for a few moments, takes a deep breath, clears his throat and decides he's going to act like he is in a court of law. He is waving his hands, putting his hands on his hips, hands on his mouth, whilst pacing up and down next to the large mahogany table.

The Zargboyans have a certain entitled confidence about them; a certain arrogance about themselves that makes other species, generally, cower before them. But for the first time, things are not going as planned and they start to look nervous. The thought of this primitive having the audacity to stand up and answer back has filled the Zargboyan lawyers with abhorrence. The nerve of this primitive, this has never happened before in negotiation meetings. They all look at Cosmo in curiosity and frustration, their smirks are no longer visible as they were at the start of the meeting.

Cosmo finally speaks, 'Right you have had your say, now it is my turn to negotiate, like you said, Mr Schmoozing lawyer.' He then looks at the Spanish looking lawyer and gives him the thumbs up. 'This is what I want all of you to do! Everyone please, attention, look at me, hear my voice and close your eyes and just listen to me carefully. No peeking, trust me.'

Some of the lawyers look at each other and at Cosmo apprehensively, in disgust. 'There is no way I am taking orders from a primitive. Closing my eyes? Is this meeting a joke to you?' Replies Model Lawyer One angrily.

'Come on now! Time is of the essence,' Cosmo says calmly, whilst pointing to his watch with a cracked bezel.

Alluca is stunned by Cosmo's request and new found confidence, but orders everyone to comply using her authoritative look. All the model lawyers again look at each other, they all back down in frustration, in fear of Alluca's wrath. Cosmo now feels able to continue, with a spring in his step.

'Right, close your eyes again. I want you to all imagine the planet you live on.'

'What, Golian 6? ''Erm, okay.' Model Lawyer Two shakes her head with confusion, but keeps her eyes closed.

Cosmo looks around to make sure all the lawyers have closed their eyes. Everyone has their eyes closed, tenderly waiting for what Cosmo has planned.

'Imagine it's perfect; your species thriving, sub-species all getting along, not only in harmony, but being efficient too. Imagine your species is being trained in contract negotiations and anything to do with law, because you're representing the sub-species on your planet and you

Zargboyans are the best at this, in fact no species even comes close. Every Zargboyan looks forward to this, as a rite of passage to adulthood and in becoming the best lawyers possible throughout the galaxy.'

At this point, Cosmo has set the scene perfectly, so all the model lawyers are now imagining their idyllic lives on Golian 6, just how Zargboyans like it.

Cosmo continues, 'So, your planet is blissful, booming; a paradise. Little Zargboyans are being trained to be the best lawyers at an early age with the dream of representing 'The KillaRhinepor Corporation' or, for some, representing other corporations elsewhere in the galaxy. Are you with me so far?'

'Yes, yes. Then what?' A few model lawyers reply, much to Cosmo's surprise.

'Then, out of nowhere, a big corporation shows up and decides to suck the resources on your planet, erm...Golian 6 in this case. This will decimate the sub-species directly, despite plans to put them in a stockroom for future convenience to distribute to other planets, losing all those potential clients on your planet. With all this disruption going on, maybe other species from other galaxies will stay away from your planet and again you have lost a plethora of potential clients externally. But that's not the really unfortunate thing to happen. No the sad thing is, the little Zargboyan children will never get to end their first negotiation contracts. Can you imagine the look of disappointment when the rite of passage does not happen? I mean, granted you will probably get other sub-species to replace those lost potential clients. But the disruption this has caused on a macro level? A whole generation of Zargboyan lawyers just wasted and thrown to do remedial 'primitive' jobs, not even intellectually challenging. All that potential, all that could have been, again wasted. Ooooof! It's chaos, pandemonium! Now, all of a sudden, you have anarchy. The world as you know it doesn't exist for this generation of unfit lawyers. The reputation of the Zargboyan species which has been built up for centuries is now in tatters. Can you imagine the negative media effect this will have on your race and other species looking at this? Other species who will be thinking to themselves, we should capitalise on this and breed, train our own formidable lawyers? Now your competing for your identity, which has been eroded because of this. Tragic, really tragic. The 'Zargboyans True Destiny' show might have to be scrapped and replaced with 'SubSpecies True Destiny'.' Cosmo is on a roll. The story telling idea came from Cosmo's dad who used to explain his crackpot theories in a story telling format for Cosmo to understand as a child.

Cosmo keeps on probing and probing. The models look terrified, even with their eyes closed it is telling for all to see.

'But the most horrific part, and I mean horrific,' Cosmo pauses.

'Wait, there is more to come?' Shouts Model Lawyer One.

At this moment, all models are showing all sorts of dreaded emotions, quite a difference from when the meeting first began. Some of the models have started sobbing furiously, fidgeting.

'No, that's not all. The most horrific part is that, it's 'your,' yes 'your' Zargboyan child that has been affected. Your child's first contract deal will never see the light of day. This generation will be a failure and Zargboyan life tarnished with its lost legacy. Can you imagine the disappointment, the shame on the family name, would you be able to look other Zargboyans in the face again? Would you be able to look at your own child the same way? That lost intellect. How would you go to work knowing everyone is looking at you, judging you as a failure in parenthood? What will your neighbours think? What will society think? The future for your child is paved with a path of pure struggle.'

Cosmo reflects on this story, as he remembered partly encouraged by his mother and father's story of when they first started to date and the barriers they had faced together. The room is silent for a moment; you can hear a pin drop. Alluca does not seem impressed, her arms folded, eyes still closed. As Cosmo looks to see what impact his story has made. Cosmo then approaches the table to ask the model lawyers a question, when suddenly...

'This is too much to take in, that story is below the belt' Model Lawyer One utters, as he stands up visibly shaken and disappears into the green mist. Remaining lawyers open their eyes, some visibly distraught, others silently shocked. Model Lawyer Three asks Alluca to be dismissed and one by one, two thirds of the model lawyers start to vanish. Model Lawyer Seven speaks to everyone, 'What is going on? This is crazy. Why am I so emotional?'

'What is this water coming out of my eyes?' Model Lawyer Two speaks up.

For the first time in Alluca's professional life, she has been impressed but remains as stern as ever. 'Bravo for the circus, Mr Griffin. Now, can we focus and get back to the contract negotiations? We still need to conclude this matter. I also humbly apologize for my colleagues' behaviour.'

Cosmo is surprised the impact his story has had on these model lawyers, as he was not expecting this type of reaction. At best it was a long shot for these lawyers to feel some empathy, to see it from his perspective. The sweating has stopped, his heart beating faster no more. Cosmo takes a look back at his silver chair and notices that it has been slightly lowered below the rest of the other model lawyer chairs in height. Almost feels like sitting in a chair at the headmaster's school office, which was another tactic they have used to make him feel inadequate, inferior, to make him sign the contract straight away avoiding confrontation. With all the mixed emotions running through his mind, he shakes his head.

He looks at his notes again with various strategies written down. Cosmo is confident as ever, ready to use his back up plans to back up plans, just like his dad drilled into him, he is not done yet.

Chapter 5 ¬ My Terms

With Cosmo's renewed confidence and sheer determination, Alluca was thinking that this is a total different Cosmo to the one that was wallowing in self-pity thirty minutes ago. *'Who is this new person, who should have been an easy pushover?* She wondered in her thoughts. *How is this possible? How dare this primitive species defy us, Zargboyans. No one treats us like this. After careful research of Cosmo's planet, this lawyer was chosen specifically because he was the easiest target to take advantage of, all the data proved this.'* She thinks, as she reflects on Cosmo.

Cosmo is bright, smart and articulate, but he has never had an opportunity to show what he can do throughout his life, for various reasons. After all the research was complied, data and records looked at, the Zargboyans thought they had found a low intelligent lawyer who they could easily manipulate and negotiate with. However, they failed to see what makes Cosmo the person he is today. This is based from his own mixed past experiences to date, which have built a resilience in him that cannot be broken and no records or data will have shown this. Cosmo just needed a push to display his attributes, what better than to confront his demons and save his planet.

The potential of Cosmo is shining through and in a firm voice he says, 'As long as I'm the lawyer of my planet, planet Earth, I will not be signing this. My terms are simple: leave Earth, the moon and our entire solar system alone. Period. Indefinitely. Furthermore, I have one question. How did you acquire my planet in the first place?' Cosmo is totally assured of himself.

Everyone remaining at the table gasps. They mutter between themselves, looking shocked, confused and taken aback with this line of questioning. The tables have now been truly turned. The remaining model lawyers seem rattled and do not know how to respond and instead they all look towards Alluca for guidance.

'I'll have to look into that,' Alluca says in a cool calm and professional manner. She then looks at the rest of the model lawyers in disdain. Cosmo can see that there is a rift between the model lawyers and Alluca developing, she is clearly not happy with their performance, but continues with his questioning.

'It's just that clause 1.36 states that if the solar system has no life forms on planets, they can be acquired. But that is 'null and void' if there are intelligent life forms to a certain standard. The technical abilities to negotiate are laid out in clause 1.36.2 and it also mentions that the planet with life forms will alone have the say on the rest of the planets in the solar system. Now, clause 4.43 is interesting. If a planet was acquired for resources and if events were to unfold where the host species are harmed in the process, then acquisition is null and void. It pauses until host species once again can have the technical abilities to negotiate.' Cosmo pauses for a few moments. He looks around and then directly to the remaining model lawyers. It seems like Cosmo is in control of the meeting for the first time and intimidating the model lawyers, who are still silent nervously watching this primitive talk. The confidence and arrogance that was shown by these model lawyers, has been fully drained, not even an insult or a reply.

'I think what happened here is you did acquire my planet many, many years ago, thousands of years ago perhaps. And an indirect consequence of this was that you destroyed my planet; all host species, dinosaurs, Atlanta, Asgard and Mount Olympus, all gone. Eventually, we homo sapiens have become the dominant species, am I correct?' Cosmo was making some points up, but he was on a roll. He pauses for a moment looking at the model lawyers directly and continues.

'And from that, our species has evolved, thereby resetting the new acquisition contract. So, your contract of owning my planet is null and void, am I correct? So, I ask you again my fellow Zargboyans: if I am the first lawyer to represent my planet, how did you acquire it? Clause 2.12 says life forms must be conscious and fully understand the decision they make and any ramifications for their host planet when signing contracts or the contract is null and void also. I see no risk assessments presented to me thus far, so again how did you acquire my planet?' Cosmo is on the offensive and is looking and feeling totally confident, pacing up and down the room with real swagger. For the first time in his life, Cosmo is in his element and is enjoying every moment of this, albeit in a surreal situation, surrounded by alien lawyers. Cosmo waits for a reaction and stands silently waiting in anticipation.

Meanwhile after listening, Alluca is now talking with her AI robot for some confirmation and clarification on the matter. Whilst this is going on, the remaining model lawyers who are sat down, are discussing quietly the situation amongst themselves.

'There is going to be a real issue back at Headquarters and can you imagine all the negative press KillaRhinepor will have? We can't afford to have another bad marketing campaign; market share is declining rapidly as it is.'

Model Five, who had stuck around, says, 'How is it even possible, that this primitive's even negotiating with us? I mean his species hasn't even figured out that nuclear energy is the most efficient source of energy around yet.'

'Never mind that,' Model Four replies. 'Alluca will have our heads for this; she looks enraged.'

'I only recently joined the firm, really, you think Alluca will reprimand or even fire us?' Model Ten asks nervously.

'She once fired the whole department because they got a single clause wrong on the Munchichi case. She's merciless, which is why she's feared throughout Sector Ten and other sectors. She's the best of the best and don't forget how she is a guest judge on 'Zargboyans True

Destiny', that's how she is in reality, ruthless. Oh, how I love that show.'

Cosmo looks and listens to them with intent, he starts again with a clear and loud voice. 'As representatives of the KillaRhinepor Corporation, do you really want that bad publicity all over the galaxy and being responsible for it?'

Looking directly at Model Lawyer Five, 'Can you imagine? Negative press, loss of revenue, loss of client confidence and so forth. By the way, I want new deeds drafted to say that KillaRhinepor is not the owner of my planet or solar system. It's free and independent and as long as I am the lawyer, this is how it shall always be.' Cosmo uncharacteristically after feeling mightily proud, does a fist bump to himself.

Alluca is shocked but is quietly impressed with Cosmo, there is something about him. 'We shall absolutely not meet your demands'. Alluca says in a formidable voice.

Alluca is interrupted by her AI assistant who transmits

information on Alluca's business card for her to read. In the space of over half an hour, what was essentially a routine procedure to obtain a signature from a loser lawyer, Cosmo has, for once, made all the model lawyers look like primitive fools, turning everything on its head. But would it be enough? Cosmo waits anxiously whilst Alluca is discussing with her AI robot. Other model lawyers are looking at each other, stunned, confused with what's going on.

Alluca starts clapping slowly, 'Bravo, bravo, Mr Griffin.'

Cosmo is stunned. He wasn't sure what was going to happen, various thoughts crossed his mind with dread. *Was he going to be tortured, experimented on or be killed for this?* Suddenly, his confidence is deflated and he starts to think about the ramification of his actions. He starts to think something even worse, maybe it is all a wild dream a simulator perhaps and nothing has come of it. But instead, Alluca calls for her AI assistant to bring pen and paper, Cian contract six and nine.

'Mr Griffin, here is your new planetary contract with everything you stipulated, no clauses or hidden sub-sections. Everything written out, exactly how you intended it to be. Now, please sign it so we can move on. I have three other meetings to get to, plus the finale of the TV show you have been hearing a lot about, from my colleagues.' Alluca looks at the rest of the model lawyers still in the same manner with disdain and shakes her head.

Alluca's AI hands over the new contract that stipulates the main points 'Cosmo Griffin will represent Earth and the solar system, until he wishes to pass on the role to another credible lawyer. Importantly, it is an independent solar system owned by no corporation. Should an untimely death occur, Cosmo's next of kin would decide who to pick as a replacement'. Cosmo reads it with great intent and signs it with glee after checking the clauses.

Alluca tells rest of the model lawyers and her AI assistant to leave and waves her hands.

'This concludes our planetary negotiation meeting,' she says, as if speaking to an audience.

Now, it is just Alluca and Cosmo alone in the room, she stares at him with those piercing green eyes.

'Never have I been outdone like this before. It is a weird feeling. Actions have consequences and consequences can have dire results, Mr Griffin. Remember this.'

Cosmo takes a gulp, 'Wow, just wow! You actually feel? This is how I feel every day. It's not great, but then you get used to it.' Cosmo replies. Alluca looks directly at him with a slight smile.

'I shall remember you, Mr Griffin.'

'Okay, but please don't kill me with laser beams or something. Can I ask you a question, what does your species actually, really, look like?' Cosmo is not intimidated by her anymore and is quite relaxed around her.

Alluca with an intrigued look laughs, 'Oh, primitive.'

She then reveals her true identity. She is a three-legged alien. Her head is the same size as a human head. Two large oval eyes are at an angle pointing to her nose with perfect long eyelashes. She has a modern hairstyle, with dark shiny blue wavy hair, coming down from a 70's style bob. She has a small cute nose, just two breathing holes and a well-proportioned mouth with red lips. Her body is slim with curves in the right places, with two long arms on each side of the body and each hand has four long fingers with perfectly painted nails to match her lips. Her skin is pearl white. She is wearing formal wear which looks like a professional business suit. When she walks, it is done effortlessly and in an elegant manner. Despite her being an alien, Cosmo is drawn to her as he sees her true beauty and personality shining through. She makes weird sounds like a dolphin, coming through her mouth. Cosmo is speechless.

'Sorry, let me re-adjust my communication. Well, what do you think?' Alluca says as she does a twirl.

Cosmo looking attentively, is bewildered. 'You look incredible, but not what I expected. Do you have super powers? Strengths? Laser beams or flying abilities?'

Alluca laughs like a little child. 'You are one funny primitive, Mr Griffin. No, no species possess any sort of special powers of the type you are referring to. There is technology available to enhance species to live, change their appearance and thrive, which is heavily regulated. But, most species prefer originality. Everyone has unique tastes; therefore no one is really ugly. However, that would be awesome wouldn't it, laser beams I mean?'

As she looks at her arm, 'I must say, I do like this watch accessory on my wrist. I might just keep this on, set a trend. We Zargboyan's normally rely on our circadian rhythm.'

'Huh, circadian rhythm?' Cosmo asks.

'Our mental capacity linked with our other senses, no need for a watch like you primitives rely on, to tell the time.' Alluca smiles and shrugs at the same time.

'Exactly, that's what I am saying, super powers.' Cosmo replies, as Alluca's AI appears again and tells her she needs to go. The AI also asks about what to do with the earbime extraction. Alluca quietly replies to her AI, 'Leave it, he has earned it.' Alluca turns back into her human form and re-establishes her professional self.

'Right, we have to go our separate ways. Our time together in this meeting has concluded. All the best, Mr Griffin. It has certainly been a memorable one.'

'Yeah. Wait, maybe we can go for a drink one day?' Replies Cosmo, but before Cosmo can get an answer he is transported back to Earth. As he opens his eyes, he finds himself lying on the park bench roughly an hour later; time it seems has not stopped and is currently running at the same pace.

Chapter 6 ¬ The Awakening

As Cosmo sits up on the park bench, he contemplates what has just happened, shaking his head. Out of all the theories he concocted whilst he sat helplessly incapacitated, meeting alien lawyers was the least unbelievable scenario he imagined. As he gets up he starts thinking to himself, *'Finally it feels like I have truly awoken. I'm still not sure if this was real or a hallucination, but from this day on, my life will change. It can't be the same, surely? All my life I had a face that was never really shown, but that stops today. If I was blind before, just sleep-walking day by day, well I have had my eyes opened with a pure clarity of thought.'*

As Cosmo makes his way home, he decides to throw the nearly empty bottle of rum in the bin next to the park bench. Cosmo has a new spring in his step. He knew what he felt must be for a reason, no going back and no negativity. No looking back at what could have been. And Alluca, how could he forget her? She was so beautiful, yet so powerful in her grace. Cosmo passes his local Korean restaurant where the owner is shouting to his employees outside again.

'Oh cool, you speak English now, that's really good.' Cosmo says. The Korean owner stops yelling and looks at Cosmo confused as he passes by. Since Cosmo was a kid, the Korean owner has always spoken in Korean and never in English. He has always been angry, even when Cosmo had a part-time job there as teenager. Cosmo thinks to himself. *'If the angry Korean owner could learn to speak English, then maybe I could do something new too.'* Unbeknown to him, he still has the earbime worms inside him, he has totally forgotten about this.

As Cosmo enters the apartment full of reflection, his parents are both watching TV together. Cosmo then walks over and stands in front of them, blocking the TV.

'Mom, Dad, I am so sorry for not being the child you expected...no, hear me out.' As Cosmo uses his hand gestures to stop them interrupting. 'You have given me love and support all the way through my life. You've always been there for me. I never actually appreciated it before and I am so sorry. Dad you and your witty crackpot, Zen theories, all invented to help me process information and it's worked. Mom, Dad I have been living a lie. I have been working as a janitor in a law firm; I'm not a lawyer. I guess I just got too comfortable. I was too ashamed to tell you guys. But that is going to change, I promise. Starting from tomorrow, I am going to start applying for proper law jobs again, even if it means starting at the bottom as a trainee or intern, it doesn't matter, I am going to try harder.'

Cosmo then hugs both of them tightly. 'I love you guys, thanks for everything.' Cosmo has a tear in his eye.

'I love you too, Cossy.' His mom replies, whilst being startled. 'We knew you were a janitor. Come on, I am your mother! You've always got our support and you could never disappoint me.' She hugs Cosmo tighter and kisses him on the cheek.

'Dude, how many drugs have you taken?' Dad jokes. 'Son, you are a decent guy, no malice in you and the best son I could ever have. Your personality could be better perhaps, I suppose, we can't have it all. But you stink; go and get a shower.' Cosmo than hugs his dad and goes to take a shower then heads straight to bed.

Both parents look at each other and are a bit confused. 'Is this puberty? Did he hit his head on the way here?' His dad says. This is followed by Cosmo's mother hitting him on the shoulder. 'Ouch.'

All through the night, Cosmo is tossing and turning, thinking about the events that unfolded during his meeting, trying to reflect on his encounter with the alien lawyers. He has just saved his planet and no one will ever find out about this amazing story, not even his parents. Who would believe him? But one thing he had proved, was the fact he did have talent as a lawyer and he wasn't a loser in his mind anymore. A little sad perhaps that no one would ever believe a story about an amazing encounter with a beautiful alien lawyer. All the barriers that Cosmo had constructed in his head came down, as he lay thinking. *Had he always been a wisher according to his dad's philosophy all his life?* All this time Cosmo would be second guessing himself, wishing for the inner confident person to come out or hesitate in making crucial decisions, it was like a whole load had been lifted. There were no limits in his mind, just an open road with clarity and clear vision. As Cosmo lay on the bed, staring at the ceiling, he imagines his inner hesitant child staring back at him with all the barriers and walls created in his mind disappearing almost like saying goodbye once and for all to his fears. He contemplates his dads ERs theory and mentally thanks his dad and goes to sleep.

In the morning, Cosmo wakes to the usual morning routine of his mom yelling, 'Cossy, breakfast is ready, go and get in the shower. Your dad is out of the bathroom now.'

'Alright!' Cosmo shouts, and despite his lack of sleep, still drowsy, he gets into the shower.

Around the same time there is a stern knock on the door from outside the apartment.

'Anybody expecting anyone?' Mother shouts as she opens the front door. She is greeted by Alluca in her human form.

'Oh, hi there. Is Cosmo Griffin here? Sorry, does he even live here?'

'Erm yes, who shall I say is asking?' Mother asks, absolutely stunned that a beautiful female is asking for Cosmo, this has never happened before.

'Sorry, where are my manners?' Replies Alluca and she shakes Mother's hand. 'I am Jenny Lucas from the Rhinemoore Corporation. Cosmo Griffin attended an interview with us yesterday and he really impressed us. Sorry, can I come in to give you more details?'

Mother is even more shocked and falling over herself with excitement. 'I am his mother! Please, come inside. Sorry for the mess. Hun, this is Jenny Lucas; she wants to offer Cosmo a job.'

'Hi, Mr Griffin.' Alluca greets Cosmo's dad, shaking his hand. 'We want to offer your son a senior position in our law firm, representing Rhinemoore Corporation and other corporate clients.'

Dad is also shocked and immediately sits down. 'Wow, just wow. Hold on, is this a prank? Where are the cameras?' Alluca chuckles to Glen's joke.

'I can assure you, Mr Griffin, this is not a prank. We were really impressed with his negotiating skills. It's customary in our organisation that if new recruits really impress, we go to their homes to deliver the good news in person. Your son is a real gem.'

Mother, seemingly out of nowhere, has made tea, got some biscuits and an old family album. She sits near Alluca all excited, 'Tell me Jenny, are you single? Tell me more about yourself?'

At this point Cosmo is finally dressed as he emerges from the shower. 'Mom, what's for breakfast? Sorry I took so long.' Cosmo yawns out loud. 'I couldn't get to sleep for ages last night, but the shower's woken me up a bit.' Cosmo grabs a cup of black coffee and takes one gulp.

'Cossy, you have a visitor, Jenny Lucas.' Mother replies.

Cosmo is confused as he turns around and he sees the gorgeous Alluca sitting there on his parents' couch next to his mom, looking at his childhood pictures. He suddenly drops his coffee on the floor in disbelief. *Was he still dreaming?* His heart is racing faster and he is staring straight at her with his mouth hanging open.

Mother gets up from the couch and comes towards Cosmo, it is an open plan apartment, shaking her head and muttering, 'Oh Cosmo, you are so clumsy. Honestly, here let me clean that up.'

Meanwhile Cosmo is walking towards Alluca hesitantly, 'Hi, erm morning, erm how are you?' Cosmo greets Alluca, slowly sitting next to her, looking curiously at her. Suddenly Cosmo's dad hits him on the head with a newspaper.

'Cosmo, where are your manners?' As his dad rolls his eyes.

'It's fine,' Alluca laughs. 'So Cosmo, after your really impressive interview yesterday, we would like to offer you a job with our Corporation, our law firm, as part of our senior team. You did really well, you should be proud of yourself.' Cosmo raises his eye brows in perplexity.

'Are you going to kill me with your laser beam?' It is the first thing Cosmo thinks of and he blurts it out accidently.

Alluca laughs again. 'You're so funny. You must get your sense of humour from your parents.'

'Humour maybe, but lack of brains and manners who knows, maybe from his mom's side?' Glen responds as he whispers to them both, hoping Jasmine does not hear. Jasmine does hear, Glen makes his way to the kitchen to grovel as she does not seem impressed.

'I don't know what to say, except thanks, it was an experience. What happens now?' Cosmo says in a hesitant manner.

'Well, for starters you will come with me to our local offices and we will get you all set up. You know, paperwork, ID, that sort of thing.'

'Do we go now? What if I say no? Are you going to kill me? Jenny Lucas?' Cosmo talks discreetly, as his heart rate returns to something like normal.

'Good question, Cosmo, how will you know if it's the right decision for you? Maybe it won't work out. That is a possibility, like anything else in life. Or maybe, just maybe, seeing if you do decide to say yes, will be the best adventure ever, something you will never experience if you never take the chance. Take the risk, Cosmo. Or you'll die wondering, what if? Think about it, Cosmo, you were scared in the meeting initially, but you persevered anyway. That is what you call courage and confidence. In reality Cosmo, nothing is in control, only your reaction is. The choice is yours Cosmo, no guarantees, but no time like the present. As for Jenny Lucas, hey, what's wrong with that name. It's the name of my teddy bear.' Alluca smiles warmly. She speaks in such a poetic manner that Cosmo is hooked.

Cosmo chuckles the thought of her with a teddy bear. *'Either I take the risk or lose the chance of a lifetime, this must be for a reason.'* Cosmo thinks to himself. 'Okay the answer's yes, I'm going to get ready, I will be two secs.'

'They are so cute together, they already have chemistry between them. I can feel it, this is so exciting! She told me she is single, maybe I can meet her parents? Too sudden?' Cosmo's mother whispers hurried sentences to his dad.

'What? She is way out of Cosmo's league! Yes dear, too sudden!' Dad says jokingly, whilst rolling his eyes.

'The Griffin men always punch way above their weight when it comes to women!' Mother responds as she raises her eyebrows and nudges him with her hips.

'Oh, Cossy make sure you also wear your dad's lucky tie, the one with an inscription at the back of it in Hindi and for heaven's sake, take that hideous broken watch off. You want to make a good impression, don't you?' She smiles at Cosmo as he passes her by.

Cosmo looks embarrassed as he half-heartedly hears them talking. 'Okay, Mom.' He goes to his bedroom quickly.

'Okay don't panic, wear your expensive cologne, take this watch off, where is my hair gel? First proper job with a bunch of aliens, yeah, no need to panic, what's the worst that can happen?' Cosmo is talking to himself in front of his bedroom mirror. He eventually gets dressed into his grey suit, white shirt and lucky grey tie. 'Looking good, shirt could have been ironed better, dad! I will do it myself next time. Do I take dad's old brief case? Nah, I shall leave it today and I think we are done here, be calm Cosmo, deep breaths.' Cosmo is still talking to himself; giving himself last minute assurances.

Meanwhile, Alluca is sitting in the lounge area of the apartment, she is taken aback with the size of living quarters and the dynamics between the Griffin family members. She really admires Mrs Griffin, the love she is showing towards Glen and Cosmo, running around the apartment cleaning, cooking, entertaining and getting ready for work. She looks at the apartment's décor and various family portraits on the walls, she can tell this family is very close to each other. The family culture might not be that different to her species she muses, as she thinks to herself.

Cosmo is ready and both Cosmo and Alluca make their way to the front door.

'Ok, we, we'll be going now,' Cosmo is all dressed up as he hurries back to the kitchen and gives his mom a peck on the cheek. 'I'm not sure when I will be back, but I'll call you.'

'Oh, Cossy, shall I make you a packed lunch?' Mom cries with a joyful pride as they both walk out the door. 'MOM, stop it!' Cosmo yells, as dad does a face palm.

Both Cosmo and Alluca leave the apartment and walk along the corridor. Alluca is trying to find the fire exit which leads to the stairs down below. She looks for the fire exit from where she arrived from. 'Come through here, we'll have a bit more privacy. Your mom seems really nice by the way.'

It is dawning on Cosmo, 'Wait! You didn't answer my question regarding are you going to kill me? Oh my god, I am really freaking out. You are real?' He pokes Alluca on the shoulder to make sure she is real, as his first reaction is still disbelief.

'Erm. Ouch! That hurts, you weirdo, we don't just kill species for no reason, that is primitive thinking,' she replies.

'Oh, I'm the weirdo? What the hell is happening? And yes, my mom is awesome.'

'Be quiet. I'm trying to get the Jauntewarpe confirmation.' Alluca holds out her business card. 'Brilliant, here we go. Stand close to me and place your thumb on this.'

Before Cosmo can reply, he does what he is told and reluctantly places his thumb on the business card. He is instantaneously transported, via a green illuminating wormhole that looks like a green neon waterfall in a tube manner. This feels like a slide, but with the person standing upright all the way through the journey. Cosmo touches the green waterfall out of curiosity; he is stunned that his hands are dry. Swimming around the green waterfall and surrounding both of them, seems to be ghostly-looking, fluorescent yellow mermaids, who almost seem to be protecting them.

'The Jauntewarpe has two functions.' Alluca shouts. 'One, is to transport anyone, anything around the galaxies, though only a select few have complete access. Some are limited to where they can travel to, but we lawyers are somewhere in the middle. The other function is to neutralise any bacteria and viruses transferring to other destinations. Germs spread from species to species can have a devastating effect sometimes. We take it for granted, but the Jauntewarpe has revolutionised travel, logistics and the perception of time among species.'

The weird, yellow translucid images flowing around us are organic souls. They are indestructible, highly intelligent beings, harnessed and infused with 'Yocto' technology. They have the ability to transcend time, distance and transport anything, anywhere around galaxies in an instant. In the past, we discovered and realised every living species has a soul, which has the capability to transcend time and space. There is no control over this and after death, the souls just get recycled back into organic matter randomly, anywhere, to any species and the cycle repeats.

Indirectly knowing this, has re-shaped and changed our philosophy, the perception of religion in some species too. Some have adapted to this information, others have struggled. How do souls form in the first place? How this happens or why this happens is still a big mystery, with theories of fifth and sixth dimensions being brandished about. But to actually harness it is a different matter. These organic souls are a little different; part souls and part tangible beings that power the Jauntewarpe, they are willing to work and breed in total harmony. This is their life.'

The whole journey feels like a minute to Cosmo, his mind and body feel stretched and weird. As Cosmo lands on the floor, his feet and legs feel all disorientated. Hitting solid ground is like the feeling of being on a treadmill for some time.

'Welcome to the Law Head Office of the KillaRhinepor Corporation, Mr Griffin. Or as we call it, the Hubris Crux.' Alluca beams with pride.

As Cosmo comes around, his body wobbling, he stares at her in disbelief and then shakes his head: there are two human forms of Alluca standing in front of him. She takes her visor off and the Alluca who came with Cosmo flops standing upright.

'What the...?' Cosmo is shocked.

'Just your standard issue Bio Drone,' Alluca says calmly. 'Unfortunately, not fully useful on your planet because of your 5G network; so much lag, so primitive. How does your species cope with such primitive technology? Right, walk with me.'

'Can I take that Bio Drone home instead?' Cosmo mutters to himself with a slight blush, looking back at the bio drone.

Cosmo takes in his surroundings, Alluca is the only alien in human form that Cosmo can see. Alluca is doing two things at once: negotiating contracts via her business card and also running her bio drone, coordinating it back to storage.

The Zargboyan species have a unique gift of literally focusing on two completely different tasks at any time and are comfortable with this. Not every Zargboyan can master this skill, as it takes time, dedication and practise. Alluca explains that Zargboyans, like primitive humans, have various jobs, but the top job in every Zargboyan's mind, their dream job, is to be a top lawyer. In their culture being a lawyer carries the highest honour. The Zargboyan skillset, genetics and culture makes them perfect candidates to be professional lawyers. This doesn't always happen, as the pressure can be too much for some Zargboyans. Cosmo is fascinated by all of this and pays acute attention whilst looking around at his new surroundings. Alluca is greeted by senior officials congratulating her on the successful Munchichi case. Alluca then turns her attention back to Cosmo. 'Are you ok, primitive? Come, let me give you the tour. You are on level sixteen, our main law headquarters at the KillaRhinepor Corporation. You made a very big impression throughout the galaxy.'

Throughout the tour, different species keep coming up to Alluca and congratulating her on winning a successful case, asking for advice and getting her signature to sign off on some important documents.

Cosmo ignoring them asks, 'How did I make a big impression?'

'Every time there is a planetary dispute, contract negotiation or hearing in our various courtrooms, the whole process is broadcast live for all species to see throughout the galaxies, as part of the Galactic Alliance

Federation's proposals for complete transparency. For some reason, you resonated with all species, which is a rarity in itself. Your particular meeting had little interest, but as soon as you started negotiating, viewing figures went through the roof and it was the most watched meeting ever, breaking all records in the process. This is probably hard for your primitive brain to comprehend, but the more views and positive responses you get equals positive ranking points, which validates the Corporation's strength throughout the galaxies. Almost like a stock market on your planet.'

'Did I boost KillaRhinepor's strength in terms of positivity ranking points?' Cosmo asks.

'No, the complete opposite. You singlehandedly affected KillaRhinepor's strength negatively. This has never happened before. Image ranking points, positive or negative have direct impacts on each corporation's fluctuating market share, which is why you have been recruited. If you were part of the problem in decreasing

KillaRhinepor's market share, you can also be a part of the solution too. It was my superior's idea to have you on board, though I'm still sceptical.'

Cosmo started to understand his role a bit more in all of this now. Still, trying to process all the details being laid bare for him, was hard to digest.

'Remember what I said before: actions have consequences and consequences can have dire results.'

As Cosmo is ignoring her foreboding tone, he continues looking around and is amazed by the vibrancy of the place and the different species working together. Small flying drones are hovering around a ceiling that appears to be a beautiful, moving, bright blue, green and purple sky with white fluffy clouds. It looks real, showing these species' true nature reflecting real night and day. Elsewhere looking around, he sees what can only be described as an open plan office but with beautiful trees, exotic flowers with different types of music blaring out of them and luminous, purple grass laid on the ground which is regenerating with every footstep. The grass covers floors fourteen, fifteen and sixteen of the structure. The perfect mix and balance between technology and nature combined in a working environment.

Cosmo is on the sixteenth floor. Both of them are making their way walking down to floor fourteen, via a moving spiral staircase. All around are offices, with no centre. There is no floor on the centre, apart from when Cosmo appears down on what would be known as, the ground floor fourteen. In the middle of the ground floor fourteen, there is a call centre type of environment, but open plan with different species all working together. A multi-species call centre with the three-legged Zargboyans all in different colours, shapes and sizes. A perfect combination of mixing nature into an office environment.

As Cosmo is walking around, he hears different species whispering to each other.

'So disgusting.'

'I thought he'd be a lot taller.'

'How do they even breed as a species?'

Cosmo blissfully ignores them; he has been called much worse in the past. Around the ground floor fourteen, there are more offices with large glass window panelling positioned all the way around the call centre. Straight ahead there is a large screen that is the size of two floors, for everyone to see. It seems to have images of famous lawyers working on different cases, with Alluca's name and face being at the top, indicating a successful win and gaining positive image ranking points for the KillaRhinepor corporation.

Also on the screen, next to Alluca's name on the right, outside of the organisation, is the ultimate group of lawyers across different galaxies who come with a feared reputation; those who have never lost a court room battle. Displaying on the screen are five names. Number 1 - Mr EKS is undefeated. The moving picture of his face looks like a cross between Satan and Dracula with three independently moving horns coming out of his head. Number 2 - Miss Ruinez, also undefeated. The moving picture of her face looks like Medusa but instead of snakes protruding from her head, there are super cute, furry looking caterpillars. Number 3 - Mr Annoose, again, undefeated. He is too hard to describe and confusing to look at. Number 4 - Mr Funnel Wet. He is also undefeated, and looks like the Egyptian god Anubis; a purple coloured jackal head with arachnid eyes. Number 5 - Miss Tuttsood is undefeated; a super seductive-looking, sleek, black tiger with zebra stripes across her face. She has the most intense, brightest indigo violet, piercing pair of eyes Cosmo has ever seen.

Alluca explains, 'There are certain lawyers you do not want to ever face. Those who have fierce reputations and play by different rules, logic, theatrics etc. I hope, Cosmo, you never meet these lawyers on that list, they can ruin you mentally and destroy your reputation and career in one courtroom appearance.'

Cosmo ponders on his new setting and is actually amazed at himself for not being totally freaked out. 'So, Alluca, are there no galactic wars raging between species or with machines? This seems so civilised. And have different species ever come to my planet before?'

'You have a weird imagination, wars? Really. What did you expect? A dystopian place where we kill each other and shout from the rooftops like primitives? And to answer your second question, different species might have visited your planet before, maybe for an ego boost, but without the necessary infrastructure in place, what is the point? Not to mention that it's illegal to visit a planet that is not part of the Galactic Alliance Federation or without appropriate documents. It's the equivalent of a sector ten planet official visiting the Antarctic on your planet and communicating with penguins to teach them econometrics. Why would you do that, what's the point? Also you might catch a native disease without knowing. Look there are approximately 356 billion stars in sector ten alone to explore, or what you might call the Milky Way Galaxy, which your planet resides in. Not all civilisations are advanced, only a sheer minority. The majority are in their infancy phase, like yours, which is not even worth colonising. The Galactic Alliance Federation believe that colonising is an outdated principle which leads to wars and what advanced civilisation wants that? The resources, the time, the costs involved, all mean it's just counterproductive. The universe is vast. History dictates empires always fall when following this ancient basic principle. We're ahead of that now and beyond petty subjugating credence. A poor philosophy in the grand scheme of things.' Alluca twirls, pointing to the achievements of the Hubris Crux.

Cosmo thinks and ponders about the Fermi Paradox, which states some civilisations are more advanced than others. Some solar systems are not even worth the time and effort for type three advanced civilisations, according to the Kardeshev Scale. *Could it be the KillaRhinepor*

Corporation is a type three civilisation, where they harness and control most of the galaxy resources? Like the sun and so on...

'Lawyers play a big part in this galaxy,' continues Alluca. 'We do the bidding of the corporations and different species we represent, and like you say, settle wars, big disputes etc. We are seen as what you might call modern day gladiators. But rather than force, we use brains and wit. To join the Galactic Alliance Federation, the minimum requirements for each planet are 100 OG (Organic Generation) network capabilities; crime rates of all combined to be below five percent of total planet population; usual progress to innovation, open trade, economic co-operation and credible representatives. Once initiated, the planet can choose which corporation it wants to be represented by, within the sector that planet resides in. Each corporation offers different incentives for each planet. A total of ten galaxies are a part of this federation and each galaxy is known as a sector. We are in sector ten. The KillaRhinepor Corporation has roughly a forty-three percent market share and declining, here in sector ten and various shares in others sectors. They provide jobs, education, infrastructure, security, prospects and much more for each planet and their species.'

'Wow, just wow!' Cosmo sighs and takes a gulp. He has a grasp of what is happening now but the sheer scale of the KillaRhinepor corporation is mind-boggling.

As they walk towards one office, both Alluca and Cosmo are approached by three Zargboyans, two of which are female twins. 'Great win Alluca! Did you like my research on the Munchichi case? Is there anything else on the new case I can help you with?' Says one of the Zargboyan twins.

'Alluca, you look nice today. It must be hard babysitting a primitive? Do you need a hand babysitting?' Asks the other Zargboyan twin, looking at Cosmo in disgust.

'Tell me something, if you're both identical twins, why is it only one of you, is actually nice looking? I'm looking at you and I'm already starting to suffer from the Troxler Effect. I expect better insults from a species like yours.' Cosmo responds as he proceeds to walk away and admire the flowers, which are somehow blaring out his favourite music. A witty response just like Cosmo's father would make do and be proud of. Twenty-four hours ago, Cosmo would have just accepted the insult with no reply, as he thinks to himself how much he has changed in such a short space of time.

'Out done again by a primitive!' Alluca says. She does not seem impressed with the three Zargboyans and rolls her eyes in disdain. She continues to walk with Cosmo. The three Zargboyans are left speechless and frustrated. Their cajoling tactic has failed miserably.

Finally, Cosmo is shown to his personal Blends, otherwise known as his office on the bottom floor. As he looks around and sees through the glass walls, he notices all the species from the bottom to the higher levels all staring at him.

'This is awkward.' Cosmo mutters

Alluca then waves her hand and the glass wall suddenly becomes a brick wall. 'Right, this is your Blends. This is where you will be doing the majority of your work from. You will be assigned an AI and here is your standard Yocto Tech business card. Please do not lose it, it holds your basic functions, transport, your wage credentials and the card is fitted with self-preservation settings. You and the business card are uniquely linked together, which you need to authorise later.'

Cosmo looks again at his office, 'So, I can change the settings to suit me, like in our original meeting?'

Alluca nods, 'Because KillaRhinepor is in need of some positive marketing.'

'Well, you can start by not making it sound like killer rhino,' Cosmo mumbles to himself.

'You are going to do charity work on behalf of our corporation. You will do pro bono work under my supervision. You know, help the little man, so to speak, and help KillaRhinepor gain some positive image ranking points, whilst increasing their declining market share.'

Cosmo agrees and nods his head, as it sounds reasonable. 'Right, can I see what it's actually like outside? I mean a paradise waterfall is great, but what's real?' He says, looking at the back wall in his office.

Alluca holds up Cosmo's business card and with a few presses, the wall at the back of the room, showing the moving paradise waterfall, disappears. There is just a vast space; he is actually in space. At a distance, he can see beautiful gas clouds that look like the nebula clouds and various planets at different distances. But these clouds are moving in slow patterns. To the right there is a small luminous orange dot. Alluca comes over and just like you would use hand gestures on your smart device, she uses the same gestures on the large window in which Cosmo is staring through. She clicks on the orange dot and enhances the image for Cosmo to see more clearly. Cosmo is amazed at the technology; it is like a smart phone, but a smart window. The sun itself, on closer inspection, seems to be in a weird cage with fluorescent blue and green lights coming out of it, which are glowing onto the enormous outer cage. It is like the lights are harnessing the energy straight from the sun. It is pretty spectacular, the sheer scale of this happening in real time.

There are various luminous spaceships travelling about and as he looks down, he can see land. The wide skyscraper Cosmo is in seems to be on a small planet.

Alluca describes the headquarters, 'It is a living, flexible working environment for professionals where they can socialise, enjoy hobbies, enjoy meals and make progress. It gives each species satisfaction in an evolving place to work and sees productivity increase massively. There are no barriers of hierarchy except for when it comes to the intellect of the individual. Some species are just genetically better in some jobs than others, sometimes it comes down to physics too, and each species accepts this and thrives.'

Alluca further explains that, 'The lower floors are filled with call centres, research and development stations, Yocto labs, interns, administrators and species just starting their careers. Levels above are mainly lead management and often where key decisions are made, but there are no barriers, as species can go wherever they please and interact with different colleagues at different levels sharing knowledge and experiences. Almost like a holacracy structured organisation but the aim remains the same, growth and expansion through building credibility by accountability. My boss, Marfa, is part of the management team, but he likes to be situated where the main lawyers are. There are hospitality suites on some of the floors, where you can go for drinks and let your hair down once in a while.'

As Cosmo looks around he stares back out of the window in a trance caused by the beautiful technological glory. There are other weird and wonderful looking skyscrapers on small planets, almost like huge asteroids linked to each other, including his. The vast scale is very impressive. Some smaller linked asteroids have huge neon lights.

'It's beautiful isn't it? The vastness of space. I sometimes stare into space looking for inspiration. These buildings are all connected. The KillaRhinepor Corporation made a principle decision many years ago to have floating space offices for travel, industry, hospitality, tourism, in fact, all sectors, away from planets so they can preserve each planet's natural beauty and environment; your basic 'polluters pay principle', where every corporation has a duty to preserving the natural world. You would like our planet, Golian 6. Its breath-taking scenery is something special, deserts filled with snow geysers, static luminous tornadoes in Lake Galian. Both of which I can see at a distance from where I live.

'Moving on, corporations are like governments on your planet; they make rules, set agendas and offer basic services to all species. If corporations are doing a great job, species will vote them in every four primitive years, one tangible way of knowing this is through the positive image ranking points and market share gained by corporations. There are always other corporations that would love to take over and it does happen all the time. The efficiency levels linked to each species have made them much more productive. The balance between work and personal life for most species is great and everyone prospers. Fundamentally, even when you look at the sheer scale of what's in front of you, there is only a finite number of resources available suited to each species needs and, as you know, appetite for demand is limitless.'

'Oh yeah, I think I read about this, the 'Malthusianism' theory,' Cosmo says.

'In basic principles, yes, but through incentivising, innovation and specialisation, most species are thriving more than ever before and we can now balance consumption rates with species' population growth rates. We have mastered this problem,' Alluca shrugs.

'Is there crime here? Also what's stopping certain individuals from buying KillaRhinepor shares and becoming a dictator on a planet?' Cosmo probes further.

'Don't get me wrong, there is crime, crime of all sorts, that will never get eliminated. But there have not been wars for centuries or serious crimes of that nature. Quite simply, if species prospers, crime reduces. Some corporations like KillaRhinepor set a base for flat business tax rate, deregulation laws, so independent, small businesses can grow and entrepreneurship can flourish regardless of revenue. Ownership of assets is crucial to this, likewise laws are in place to protect species and stop enfranchisement, meaning there are no shares to buy at KillaRhinepor,' no states or dictatorships can form from this. Every species has a duty and a choice, you can get a job, up skill yourself, become an entrepreneur, maybe one day become a corporation, like KillaRhinepor did with its Yocto technology. At every point in one's career, a person is rewarded. But you only pay one flat working tax. Anything that is not profitable is given the most support through tax and revenue generated. Full disclosure and transparency where the funds are distributed, through efficient supply-side policies is key, because to KillaRhinepor accountability is essential. Imagine whole new markets opening up throughout sector 10, the possibilities. All species have a duty of care and buy into this philosophy. That is the KillaRhinepor way in a nutshell.' Cosmo is stunned just trying to take this vast information in. 'With opening up to galaxies through efficient travel and communication methods, species no longer overall strive for power. Once you realise the mentality of power is worthless, you start enjoying life. You have whole galaxies to explore, now imagine the ability you have to experience all this, the scope and opportunities are endless, beyond a species' lifetime span.'

Through the window he sees all sorts of drones and small spaceships coming towards him. It is the galactic press, who want to take pictures of Cosmo, almost like the paparazzi. Alluca intervenes and summons the KillaRhinepor security. Out of nowhere spaceships surround the press and usher them on.

'Wow was that for me? Am I famous?' Asks Cosmo excitedly.

'No you're not famous in that sense. Think of it, like a new attraction at a zoo.' Cosmo squints his eyes at Alluca, as he is not impressed with that remark.

Upon reflection, Cosmo is amazed. It is nothing like the violence and disorder he imagined space would be like as a kid or watching on TV. Instead, everything works in tandem, peace and harmony. Cosmo is excited to see what more is out there, still trying to take it all in.

Whilst Cosmo is distracted watching space, 'Right, that reminds me, swallow this.' Alluca says.

Before Cosmo can ask what it is, Alluca shoves something in his mouth via a gun device. A capsule with another worm inside is administered through force into his mouth.

Just then Cosmo immediately drops to the floor and grabs his head. 'Oh my God this hurts! The pain is getting worse; I think my head is about to explode! Alluca you have killed me!'

Alluca, with her AI who has appeared, does some diagnostics using her business card. 'Oh, quiet, Cosmo. No one has been killed, yet! Quickly AI, can you scan and spot the eyebime?''Primitive, you will die in ten seconds of a brain aneurysm unless you hold on and relax.' The AI responds.

'There it is! AI, please extract it now and circulate normal blood flow.' Alluca says authoritatively. The AI's hand has become surgical tools and partially takes out the bloated slimy black and purple worm from the side of Cosmo's eye with laser precision, then injects his brain with special liquid to counteract the effects and circulate blood flow.

Cosmo is picked up from the floor by the AI, who sits him on the fine leather couch. The AI disappears back in Alluca's business card.

'What the hell happened?' Cosmo asks. 'What was that disgusting worm type thing? Am I going to die? No man should ever have to suffer that pain, ever.'

Alluca rolls her eyes. 'Relax, you will be fine.' She presses some pressure points on Cosmo's head and all of a sudden Cosmo feels a lot better, more like himself again.

'Basically you've got access to breathing and hearing through the earbime worms we planted in our initial meeting, but no access to your illusion senses. Your primitive little brain cannot handle it. So every species you encounter will see you as a primitive and not a species that reflects theirs. Also, you will see their true form and not human form.' Alluca further explains.

'We ingest the eyebime worm, because it creates better communication between species. These are the most sophisticated worms you will ever come across. These disgusting things, as you refer to them, make everyone linked and synced across the galaxies, like the social media, internet connection on your planet, so communication between species can be synonymous and seamless. Your physical, verbal communication is uploaded to the Nebula via the ear/eyebimes, then beamed down to the person you're trying to communicate with, a two-way channel. Sort of like the cloud system, you use for data storage on your planet. The only difference being, we have surpassed that with technology and organic matter now being infused, with pure efficiency right across all ten sectors.' Alluca tries to explain.

'Wow, just wow. Kurzweil's theory on law of accelerating returns is right, this is awesome, I have super powers.' Cosmo says enthusiastically.

'I can see the advancement of technology is making you animated like a child. It's weird seeing it through the eyes of a primitive, fascinating. I guess we just take it for granted.' Alluca shrugs.

'Pay attention, Cosmo! Your primitive brain can only handle some elements of this, evolution has played a cruel trick on your species it seems. You still will be able to understand different languages, see written languages, communicate with different species and breathe in different climates without realising, but not in space obviously. Without your illusion senses, this might be a challenge for you when communicating with other species as you look repulsive to other species and let's say displeasing on the eye. Please know I'm sharing this information, because I respect your intelligence.' Alluca's last sentence is said in a witty manner.

As Cosmo looks around, he notices a hologram screen on the side wall of his office displaying a TV commercial for the latest earbime worm infused with up-to-date Yocto technology, which can change voice patterns and help acclimatisation faster in different environments. It seems to be endorsed by Alluca and famous lawyers from the past.

Cosmo tears himself away from the advert and realises Alluca has been a bit rude. 'Hey, what's wrong with the way I look? I mean, plenty of people think I'm handsome, my mom being one of them and she counts. Oh, I see you're still bitter regarding our first negotiation meeting and here's me thinking it's because of my good looks and charm,' Cosmo has a cheeky smile.

'Please, just don't go there.' Alluca says in a dismissive way, giving him the hand gesture treatment.

Cosmo asks another question, 'Do species... I mean is there such thing as interspecies relationships. I mean that would be weird when you find out actually they are totally different, wouldn't it?' Cosmo says curiously.

Alluca looks at him and raises one of her eyebrows, 'Interspecies having relationships happens all the time. It was once frowned upon, and is still a taboo subject in some manner, but now it is more accepted in certain species, certain societies. Sometimes genetics and sheer physics prohibit this from happening which can cause emotional distress. Even with these barriers, some interspecies relationships do make it work regardless and flourish. But you don't need to worry about that with your looks. Right, can I continue now?' Alluca thinks of Cosmo like a child who cannot stop asking questions.

Cosmo pauses for a few seconds and gestures silently to suggest 'Please continue,' in a witty response.

Alluca passes the business card to Cosmo again. 'This is your life. Your wages, identification, transportation using the Jauntewarpe, and AI are all on there. Oh, I forgot. Please meet your personal AI. AIs assist you with your day-to-day tasks. Thanks to Yocto technology, a bit like your Nano technology theory on your planet but much more advanced, these AIs can take solid form or go back into a virtual digital state in the 'Hub' when you don't need them.' Alluca can be seen doing some calculations on her business card.

'Erm, I have another question. Don't AIs want to take over eventually and rule the universe?' Cosmo asks.

Alluca bursts out laughing with the sheer amount of unusual questions from Cosmo, 'Possibly? But what is the end goal for AIs? We have established rules and laws to co-exist, they have their own universe. Without species AIs have no purpose. There might be rogue AIs out there but they are governed by the AI Architects who control and manage the AI universe.' Alluca answers with a smile.

As if to demonstrate, just then Cosmo's AI pops out of his business card and it's Alluca's AI from the first meeting and the AI who has just helped get the eyebime out of him. Only this time she is in a strop and not acting professional at all. It is like this AI has had a personality transplant.

'Do I have to be his AI? He is so primitive, with weak brain power. Can't I still be yours, Alluca? Pretty please! If not, Well, I'm just going to go back to Hub City then.' The AI folds her arms and is staring at the ceiling in protest.

The Hub or 'Hub City' is the AI universe, a vibrant place that looks like a tropical island full of colour and crystal-like buildings. This is where all AIs congregate in a virtual city, if they are not on assignments or being summoned. Each AI has their own personality developed overtime through the people they work with and experience. AIs do not sleep, eat and never take rests, instead they continue to do research in their own Hub City libraries following pursuits that match their personalities. Some AIs, the ones that are not on assignments have intellectual debates with other AIs in cyber cafés. They meet up with other AIs and talk about the complexities of being an AI, discussing the principles of AI law, ethics, similar to Asimov's 'The Three Laws of Robotics'. There are other AIs even protesting outside Hub City Square demanding rights for AIs to choose their own names rather than be known as a number, they can be heard shouting with placards "Say no to AI'ism". Other AIs can be seen looking at them in disgust whilst walking past them.

'Get a job?' Says one AI walking past.

'No, you sir, check your AI privilege?' Replies an AI protester.

Alluca calmly looks at her AI. 'I'm sorry, I have orders, but I will still be around, your primary concern is for Cosmo and secondary is for me.' The AI is acting like a spoilt teenager and goes onto her holographic screen beaming from her stomach and sits down on the couch in a huff.

Cosmo notices her frustration, 'Okay then. Erm, hi AI,' He notices there is writing across her chest and it has changed to L23UC1ll310. 'You know what? I am going to call you Lucille. Hi Lucille, how's it going? Me, I'm great, thanks for asking. Who's your favourite person? Cosmo, yeah?' Cosmo attempts to entertain Lucille and is rewarded with a little smile, as if to say she likes her new name and a wave before she goes back into her mood with her arms crossed. Cosmo then turns his attention back to Alluca thinking inquisitively.

'You know what Alluca! I am going to need a historical specialist, thinking about it unless Lucille can help? Some kind of old AI expert, who can tell me the complete history of your world and the other species in detail. I need this to help me understand the species I will be dealing with and representing. If I can't communicate with them more effectively, this will give me a better insight. If they see me in human form they might run away or you know be repulsed by me, those were your words.' Alluca rolls her eyes again.

'Well, AI's have some capacity for history but not what you want and I can't argue with your logic. Let me have a look. Most historian AIs were decommissioned and destroyed because there is no use for them. Oh wait, I have found one that might be available in our artefact library. All artefacts are preserved in Yocto technology which is a big bonus. Let me just transfer and reactivate it. I just need confirmation. ..Brilliant, it's all yours Cosmo.'

Suddenly another AI pops up. This one is a three-foot bronze and steel covered retro looking robot. There is smoke coming out of its big chest. It looks like an old-fashioned butler, but in the middle of a mid-life crisis, as he is wearing a steel snapback cap backward. The AI has two small skis attached at the bottom and is hovering with no feet. A distinguished steel box goatee beard, seems to have its own personality judging by the illuminous lights reflecting off it. His body has three arms, all with white gloves. On his chest is written T3J346M910.

'Reporting for duty, Sir. I am beholden to you, Sir,' he says like an excited child full of energy. 'I am so proud and it is an honour, Sir to be working with you and handling your requests. Can I just say, Sir...?' There is a glitch and on his stomach appears a bar which seems to be informing Cosmo that something is downloading. After the glitch and the downloading has finished, the AI continues where he left off. 'That you are looking spectacularly handsome today? As a historian, what can I record for you today? What history can I look up for you today?' The new AI seems to be very joyful. Cosmo looks at this new AI's chest.

'You know what, I am just going to call you Tej. I like your positive attitude.' Cosmo says whilst looking at Lucille.

'Oh thank you, Sir. I have never been given a name before. Actually I can't remember still waiting for information to download. This is the start of a fruitful working relationship, I'm sure.' Lucille looks at Tej in disgust and rolls her eyes just like Alluca does.

'Right, this is what I want you to do Tej: start downloading all the histories of our potential clients, their ancestors, the whole lot. Lucille, can you transfer the necessary files to Tej for this to happen?' Cosmo asks.

Lucille rolls her eyes. 'Done.'

Just then, there is a shout from Alluca who has been distracted by other Zargboyans looking at the screen outside the office. 'Guys, come here!'

As everyone leaves the office, they look towards the big screen on the wall. On the screen is Cosmo Griffin's name which has appeared with a case name attached: The Gauwladykes, case number 23232425. Everyone is looking around and turn their focus on Cosmo. Cosmo is confused thinking to himself, *okay it's the first case. What is the big deal?*

'Everyone get back to work,' Alluca yells. 'Guys, get back to your office, I will be back.'

As Cosmo and the AIs walk inside the office, Cosmo is looking confused.

'Can you turn the top half of the wall to a window setting, facing the call centre and offices?' Cosmo asks Lucille, who obliges.

Cosmo spots Alluca on the second floor and she is really busy with species of all sorts, making important decisions. In Cosmo's mind, time seems to go in slow motion as he admires her from afar; a little part of him is falling for her each time he sees her. He is daydreaming looking at her in action.

'Alluca, always rubs her nose when she is stressed. That is so cute. I wonder what kind Zargboyan she likes or do you think she is into interspecies relationships, Tej?'

'I have checked Sir; it seems Alluca is a private person. Even if I was to research her past I would need her permission,' replies Tej.

'No, not like that Tej, that's kind of a little stalker territory. I mean her hobbies, interests, friends, what she likes in a partner. Alluca can have anyone. I can imagine the demand to date her is extremely high. Damn, supply and demand sucks sometimes.' Cosmo and Tej both nod their head in agreement. Lucille is not impressed with either of them.

Lucille suddenly gets up and moves towards them both, still gazing at Alluca attentively.

'You will never be able to date her; you do realise that don't you? Many have tried. The odds of that happening are exactly 1.2 trillion times to one, Cosmo, which is also how many times better than you she is. She is perfection in every way.' Lucille is quite protective of Alluca. It seems they have had a great working relationship for a long time.

'Wow. Just wow! So precise, 1.2 trillion times, really?' Cosmo replies shaking his head, raising his forehead.

'Don't worry, Sir, you are two trillion times better than anyone in this building.' Tej speaks in an authoritative way.

'Erm, thanks Tej.' Cosmo replies in a voice that reflects his awkwardness about Tej's devotion. Cosmo quickly turns back to Lucille.

'Tell me something, if my Illusion senses didn't work, then why is it I can still see Alluca in her beautiful human form? I mean I am not complaining!' Cosmo asks Lucille who looks perplexed.

'What? Let me check, this has not happened before, ever. I will have to do an analysis of this.' Are you sure you can't see Alluca in her true form?' She asks Cosmo firmly.

'Nope she is in her human form, looking stunning as ever.'

Lucille comes over to do a full brain scan, but is baffled as to how it is possible.

'Since our first meeting I have been seeing Alluca in her human form, granted it was probably the bio drones or Blends sensory illusion system, but even with the eyebime taken out, I see her in her human form.'

Just then Lucille and Cosmo are side-tracked and interrupted by three Zargboyans again, who tried to suck up to Alluca to no avail. They enter his new office looking angry and disgruntled.

'This used to be my office,' One of them says aggressively, seeming to know Cosmo. 'We have all been demoted because of you. We are now glorified researcher and paperwork administrators.'

'We were in primitive form. This one will not recognise us,' says one of the twins.

'Oh wait, I remember you guys from the meeting. Why should I be responsible for your incompetence?' Replies Cosmo, in a confident manner. Now and again we see Cosmo's confidence come out in small doses.

'Bravo, Sir. Well replied, Sir. Would you like a neck massage?' asks Tej. Cosmo looks at Tej in a weird way.

'No!' Cosmo turns to the Zargboyans. 'Look you guys, I was just doing my job, no hard feelings. If anything, it was me that was really impressed by you. You guys were awesome.'

Cosmo tries to shake their hands. A male Zargboyan refuses to shake his hands. 'We will see how long you last. The Gauwladyke case? Ha, you have no chance! Mr Annoose will destroy you mentally piece by piece, make you look like the primitive fool you are. It's our dream to face such feared lawyer opposition. I will dance when you collapse and embarrass yourself at the Intergalactic court of Omens.'

'Wow, an actual form of species-ism. Is that even a word? Did I just invent a word, Lucille? I remember you!' Cosmo turns to face the male Zargboyan. 'Weren't you the one who first cried all over the place in our initial meeting? And you were the first Zargboyan to leave the meeting, when I told you my story, you ran out like a gushing child? Also, what is that you're wearing, a yellow earbime sponge look alike thing, which doesn't match your face and does not do any justice to your body by the way.

Well, it's been great knowing you, I shall cherish our time together. Now please leave my office, though come again for drinks sometime.'

Cosmo ushers them out as Lucille receives a phone call relayed from planet Earth.

'Come on Cellinska, he doesn't know fashion, take no notice of the primitive.' Says one of the Zargboyan twins who puts her arm around him, who seems to be a little upset by Cosmo's mean comments.

Cosmo raises his eye brows, hands on his hips and is dumbfounded, *what a hissy fit, that was easy*, he thinks to himself.

'You have a call Cosmo, from your mom; do you want to take it?' Lucille puts up a hologram of the phone call.

'Oh! Hi, Mom. I am just busy right now...going into an important meeting.'

'Oh it's okay, Cossy I was just making sure you're okay and have had lunch; you got to keep your health up now you've got a new job. And how is Jenny? Is she with you? Is she there?'

'Mom, not now, you're being embarrassing. I'm fine really, but busy. Got to go.'

'Okay, Cossy, see you home soon. Love you. Wait! Did you know that the Rhinemoore Corporation is the largest law firm on the west coast? And not far from LA. I'm so proud of you. Tell Jenny I can make her dinner one night.'

'Mom please! Yeah, I knew that about the Rhinemoore Corporation, Mom. Love you. Goodbye.'

Cosmo pretends not to see Lucille, as she can be seen giggling as she turns off the hologram projector.

Meanwhile, back at home Jasmine looks at Glen 'I think our Cossy just farzeed me.'

'It was only a matter of time, Hun!' Glen responds, laughing to himself. He is not laughing for long, as he is punched on the shoulder by Jasmine. 'Ouch.'

Chapter 7 ¬ Home-working

As Cosmo ponders, he asks Lucille a question. 'Lucille, that is a good point my mom just made. How is it that the Rhinemoore Corporation is a real firm? I don't get it.'

Lucille folds her arms, evidently thinking it is a stupid question, rolling her eyes. 'Look Cosmo, you are basically a silent shareholder, a majority shareholder, of three of the largest law firms, as your mom says, on the west coast. They are now combined into one known as the Rhinemoore Corporation. The process is still going through as it takes forever for processes to conclude on your planet. But your ownership has been backdated six months thanks to your primitive technology, which we hacked and managed to develop a legit history with date of incorporation etc. You'll have to have some patience about your wages. You can't use the funds yet, as I'm still working on a paper trial. Once the transfer happens from Roobal Credits to your local currency, it will trigger alarms to your local authority, the FBI and all the banks. The exchange rate will be vast as your planet is like an infant third world country compared to ours respectively. This is to be expected but with the paper trail backtracked, it will be fine.'

Cosmo slowly understands some of what Lucille is saying and nods his head as acknowledgement.

'We had to make this transition happen in the most efficient and logical way possible. This is the best outcome; it will allow you to work for the KillaRhinepor Corporation and still maintain a legit story at your primitive home and being your own boss, gives you the flexibility to strategically handle workloads. I have already composed your work history profile, in case people want to look you up. I will also send out details of when your father can get invaluable medical treatment for his chest. The only problem will be, telling your parents about your ownership of the Rhinemoore Corporation. I'm not a social worker, I can't sort your personal life out too, you know.' Lucille waves her hands in the air in frustration having to explain all of this to Cosmo.

'Wow, so mean, you hurt my feelings Lucille,' Cosmo says jokingly.

'Hurting your feelings makes you think harder, Cosmo, keep paying attention. Plus, I enjoy hurting your feelings!' Lucille says with a fake smile.

Cosmo gulps and takes a seat behind his desk slowly. Every second he seems to be bombarded with awe-inspiring news and information of some sort. 'This is crazy. I own three of the largest law firms? Oh my God, that is awesome! With great power, comes … oh never mind.' That exchange rate thing, I have no idea, Lucille what you are talking about. So I am a legit owner of these law firms. Wow, just wow!'

For AI's the notion of time is irrelevant because they can get so much done within seconds, however minutes and hours feel like a lifetime for these advanced robots and sometimes they do not take into account the impact, time has on certain primitive species. Lucille looks at him directly.

'Have you calmed yourself down, your heart beat has slowed down again which seems to insinuate you have? Right then! You have an official meeting with the Rhinemoore board in one hour, then every day following. I will update your schedule and movements for Alluca and Marfa to see. On the fourth day, you will officially meet the senior team and have a proper induction at KillaRhinepor.'

Cosmo is stunned and takes another gulp, shaking his tie. Everything is going at breakneck speed. There is a lot of information to process and take in.

'Wait you can see my heart beat? I feel so violated.'

Cosmo shakes his head again, 'Hang on, rewind. I have a

meeting with the board in one hour? Lucille could you not, erm maybe, I don't know, given me more time to prepare? How do I get there? What do I say? What do I wear? I have so many questions.' Lucille does a face palm and shifts to a different soft, tone of voice.

'Yes I can see your heart beat; in fact, all your organs are working efficiently, simple hourly bio scanning is a routine function of mine. It's a horrible job but someone has to do it, to make sure you are working at optimal capacity. On a side note, your bowel movements are fine too, so no problem there going into this meeting,' Lucille giggles to herself. 'I have taken care of everything; just don't lose your business card. I have arranged transportation to the meeting and I will be available via your smart phone. I would go there with you, being your personal assistant, but you still run on primitive 5G network. Tell me when you want me to leave and I shall make the arrangements. Remember you have back to back meetings for three days at three of your law firms. You are merely introducing yourself. Please don't do anything stupid.'

Cosmo calms himself down, relaxes his body, 'So whole body scan huh. Hey can you please leave my bowls out of this, what is it with you and Alluca regarding my bowl movements? Well I guess now is as good as any time to go.'

Lucille makes some calculations on the projector coming out of her stomach, which flashes green and yellow holographic images. 'Okay, place your thumb on your business card.'

'Why always my thumb?' Cosmo can't help himself asking so many questions, much to Lucille's frustration.

Lucille stands like a teenager with her hands on her hips and the two other hands from her head waving her fingers at Cosmo. 'Why so many questions? Let me explain this once, each finger acts as a different function when you press on the business card. The thumb print is always for travel, duh. The forefinger or index finger is to access work files or any other explicit information you need. For security, wage and self-preservation mode, your middle finger is used. Your ring finger or fourth finger is for your personal file usage and for your little finger that is for another day. Why Cosmo? because the algorithms in your primitive brain, now indicate you are distracted, Cosmo! You have stopped listening to me and you're not paying attention are you? Why oh why, do I put up with this. I'm going go back to Hub City and joining in with the protests, there has to be more to life then working with a primitive, surely?' Lucille says frustratingly.

Cosmo stops being distracted from all the features around him in his personal office. This office, which is more unbelievable than he could ever have dreamed of, is something he has never had before, never mind that it is an alien one. He shrugs his shoulder to suggest an apology, he presses his thumb on the business card, to avoid hearing Lucille shout again and is immediately transported via the Jauntewarpe to a public toilet cubicle back on CX321, also known as Earth. Cosmo feels a bit less disorientated this time. As he opens the door, a small teenager, is staring at him in amazement. Cosmo does the shush finger at him and runs out of the men's room, tidying his suit and tie up at the same time.

Cosmo is confused to find himself in an airport. he slowly walks out of the main exit and recognises it as his local airport. Slowly walking through the airport, he is still not sure what he is meant to be doing. As Cosmo walks out of the exit, he notices a driver holding a placard with his name on it.

'Hi, that's me, Cosmo Griffin.' The chauffeur looks curious, as though he does not really believe him.

'Sorry, you need my ID,' Cosmo says. He pulls out his wallet and hands him his driving licence.

The chauffeur immediately apologises. 'I'm so sorry, Sir. I thought you be a lot older and be with your entourage. Do you have any bags, Sir?'

'Don't worry about it, just me. And no, I travel light.'

'Of course, Sir'.

The chauffeur nods and shows Cosmo to the car, a 'Toyota Century Royal' limousine is waiting for him. Other chauffeurs waiting for their clients are looking at the car and taking pictures. They both sit in the car and drive off. On the way to the meeting, Cosmo ponders how much his life has changed in a matter of twenty-four hours and how much he has changed as a person. He has gone from seeing himself as a loser and creating barriers in his mind constantly, to being driven by a chauffeur in a photogenic car, being called sir and now was on his way to a meeting with the board of the biggest law firm on the West Coast. He starts to think about how he will act at these meetings; cool, calm and collected or be himself just more confident, more extrovert maybe.

'Tell me something, driver, what's your name?'

'Tom, Sir, Tom Greenman.'

'Please call me Cosmo, Tom, I can't be dealing with this sir stuff.'

'No problem, Cosmo. You know, you are totally different to how I expected you to be.'

'Really, in what way?' Cosmo is intrigued.

'I was told how ruthless and extremely intimidating you are, if you don't mind me saying and how important you are to the corporation. I mean come on, you're sat in a car, of which only four have ever been built, it is mainly used for head of empires. I had to do all sorts of checks and training just to drive this particular car!' Says Tom, in an upbeat manner, as he feels privileged to be driving this vehicle.

'Nah, I'm not ruthless. It's just an exaggeration, like Chinese whispers, I guess I should be humbled to sit in this car.' Cosmo is a bit stunned, thinking how his dad would love to be sat in here also.

Suddenly, Cosmo gets a call on his smart phone. He answers it, to hear Lucille's voice.

'Hi. I have been acting like your Personal Assistant and contacting the firms on your behalf, giving them a full description of who you are, your profile details, what you expect, etc. Just remember to be silent. Don't give much away in the meeting and please don't be yourself, in fact don't say anything at all.'

In the background, Tej can be heard saying, 'Sir is going to smash it at the meeting, nothing to worry about. Be yourself, you're fantastic Sir.'

'What is this meeting about?' Cosmo asks. 'What do I do? I haven't got any notes.'

Lucille answers in a frustrating voice, 'Look, Cosmo, you don't take notes to the meeting. You set meetings and everyone else does the work for you. Just be quiet and nod your head at an angle. Oh, this is so going to be a complete disaster.'

'Have faith in Sir, he is the best!' Tej can be heard in the background, full of confidence.

'Thanks for the vote of confidence. I have to go.'

'We have arrived, Cosmo. Enjoy your meeting,' says Tom as he parks the car.

'Can you do me a favour, Tom, and stick around to take me home after I finish with this meeting? Is that okay?'

'No problem.'

Tom opens the door for Cosmo and is greeted by two members of staff who usher Cosmo inside the building.

'Welcome! How was your journey? Can I get you anything to drink? A light beverage perhaps?'

'We have put on a presentation for you, Mr Griffin.' There is a line-up of what seems to be all of the firm's staff.

Cosmo shakes the majority of their hands. Everyone is smiling, some with nervous smiles.

'Please, this way, Mr Griffin.'

As Cosmo enters the boardroom, he finds a table bigger than his parents' apartment surrounded by high level executive partners from around the world and high-ranking lawyers, all waiting for him. As everyone takes their seat, he is directed, ushered to the head of the table so he can see the full presentation. Never in Cosmo's wildest dreams could he have imagined being sat here among these high ranking professionals, the elites in a top law firm and around the world. The presentations commence. One by one they start to talk about profit levels, rebranding the Rhinemoore Corporation and marketing strategies.

The Japanese partners are speaking among themselves in Japanese. 'The return on investment will be huge and long-term prospects seem very good indeed.'

'I agree especially with Mr Griffin, who helped our Japan offices. We have now become dominant players in the Asia Pacific region.'

'You know, that's a very good point you make; the long-term prospects are growth and expansion and I appreciate your acknowledgement.' Cosmo responds, thinking it must be one of Lucille's doing.

They and others sat close by, look impressed because to them Cosmo speaks in fluent Japanese, even though to Cosmo this seems all natural.

The Japanese partners tell Cosmo, 'We hope you liked our limousine gift.'

'Thank you, much appreciated.' Cosmo says whilst slowly nodding his head at an angle.

The presentations continue with talk about the nuclear power plant project located in a small town near Nevada and how it will create thousands of jobs. This is laying the ground work for future expansion. There was still a possibility of a publicity backlash, but they discussed how they will overcome this. Everyone is clapping and looking for Cosmo's approval. It occurs to Cosmo that there is a distinct parallel world where Cosmo feels he is a small insect at KillaRhinepor Corporation, with the epic scale of it all, but here, he is like a king of the castle and everyone is looking to him for leadership and guidance in approval. Here he makes all the important decisions.

After the presentations are done, Cosmo slowly stands up and claps. 'Well done, I am impressed. Continue the good work.'

There are cheers all around the boardroom. They seem proud of themselves for putting together a good presentation in an extremely short timescale.

'Can I take a look around and speak to the ground staff?' Cosmo asks.

High ranking partners, Kitony, Logan and Mariyah, all look a bit puzzled but agree. 'We will personally show you around.'

'Good work, everyone. I mean it. Shall we?' Cosmo says in a confident manner. As they leave the office, there is a sigh of relief among the staff, who talk amongst themselves.

'He seems nice, younger than I imagined.'

'So young to have all that power and money.'

'Seems quite level-headed.'

The partners and Cosmo walk around, discussing who does what and where. As Cosmo is walking around he is spotted by a couple of people who recognise him from high school.

'I can't believe that is Cosmo! From high school. Do you remember him? He was very quiet and a bit weird.' They both get on their smart phones and research him.

'Oh my God! There is a Wiki page on him. It says he made some investments and it rapidly turned into success and steamrolled from there. His net worth is undisclosed but it is said to be in the region of $Billions'

'It's like everything he touches turns into gold and success.' As Cosmo passes them by, he is oblivious to them.

The partners take him to meet the ground staff, who are the researchers, interns and general administrators. Cosmo looks at the staff and says, 'Hi guys, can I have everyone's attention. Nice to meet you all, there will be a few changes, but I need your help. Tell me about your jobs? Do you like it or don't like it? How can we improve your job, if so?' Some of the staff come over and decide to have a chat.

'Yeah I like working here,' said one.

'Sometimes the workload can get overwhelming, but it's nothing we can't handle,' another shrugged.

'Hopefully, there are prospects to move up the ladder here.'

'Thanks for your honesty, much appreciated,' Cosmo replies. 'Can we make sure there is a programme available for these staff to progress? They are the future. Also can we ensure from next week onwards, all lawyers and senior management staff come and spend a day here once a week. I want to get rid of this hierarchy mentality? We need to understand what it's like to work at ground level and learn from this. Sometimes I think we forget where we are and can become a little narrow minded.' A few ideas he has picked up from the KillaRhinepor Corporation.

The partners look at each other in surprise. This is not what they were expecting. 'Yeah, sure. We will definitely arrange that asap, anything else?' says Mariyah.

'Oh and another thing; there will be no redundancies because we will be better and more efficient with staff who're not constantly watching over their backs. We need to get rid of this cut-throat type of culture and reward achievement and merit', Cosmo says with confidence. 'I need to go now but, again, keep up the good work.'

'That's great news, thank you.' The partners chorused.

As all walk towards the entrance, Cosmo spots Tom, the chauffeur, who is waiting for him. 'It's been a pleasure,' Cosmo says, shaking everyone's hands.

Tom opens the door as Cosmo climbs in the car, Toms asks 'Where to next and how was your meeting, Cosmo?'

'The Adelph Complex on St Anne's Drive. Yeah, the meeting went well as expected' Cosmo answers. 'Tom, do me a favour please and put some nice music on, a bit of progressive house music, please. It helps me think and get focused.'

Tom puts the music on as they drive to their destination. Cosmo's phone starts to ring again.

He answers the phone, it is Tej; he is ecstatic. 'Sir, you were brilliant, you smashed it, Sir. You were cool, calm, composed, I always knew it. You were amazing!' Lucille can be heard in the background arguing with Tej to let her speak.

'You were average, definitely could have been better. Maybe next time just be quiet and think before your primitive brain speaks. We circumnavigated the building's security cameras and your smart phone to check in on you.'

'You sound like my parents. Look, I'm heading off home. I need a rest,' Cosmo says petulantly.

'And rightly so, Sir. You get some bed rest, Sir,' says Tej in the background.

'Oh yes, the primitive brain needs eight hours sleep minimum to recharge. Bye!' Replies Lucille, hanging up. Cosmo continues to listen to the music on the drive home.

'We are here, Cosmo. Would you like me to wait?' Asks Tom, looking confused at the modest apartment complex.

'No, this is my home. See you tomorrow.' Now, Tom looks really confused. How can a person who owns three major law firms live here?

'Okay, Cosmo. I'll be here in the morning.' Looking bemused.

Cosmo stares at the apartment complex and reminisces, his apartment might have been small, but it had seen so much heartache, yet also so much love over the years. As Cosmo walks into the apartment he is greeted with hugs and kisses from his proud parents.

'We are so proud of you! Tell me all about your first day. How was Jenny? Is she coming over soon?'

'Mom, please! It was a normal day at work. I'm just trying to get used to processes they use.' As Cosmo squirms under the embarrassing attention.

Cosmo's dad intervenes, 'Hun, let Cosmo breathe. Son you did good. Now go and sort yourself out.'

'Cheers, dad.' Replies Cosmo, as he walks into his bedroom from his first day at work, shattered. All the new information he has to process is whizzing inside his brain. He collapses on his bed, and contacts Tej by accident, whilst experimenting, by placing his ring finger on the business card. He eventually falls asleep.

The following day, Tom picks Cosmo up, he is feeling all refreshed in his light blue suit and tie. He picks up his dad's old briefcase and Tom takes him to the next meeting. Cosmo is again greeted by all the main players at the second law firm and the presentations continue all day. Cosmo again thanks them for their hard work. He explains that he wants a training programme in place for all staff and for the lawyers, senior and management staff to work one day a week with the interns, administrators and researchers, creating a new business culture at the Rhinemoore Corporation.

The same happens on the last and third day of his introduction meetings. The processes are the same, all day meetings and presentations to follow. Towards the end of the third day, a hesitant personal assistant speaks to one of the senior partners in the meeting, who then reluctantly hands Cosmo something discreetly. Cosmo is shocked, he has so many emotions, which come flooding back from his past. He apologises to the presenter and asks them to continue the presentations without him, as he leaves the boardroom. The personal assistant walks with Cosmo and directs him to the lobby. Where a woman and her daughter wait to speak to Cosmo. As Cosmo opens his hand, it is a badge with W etched on it, he cannot believe it, after so many years. It is Sofia and her little daughter. As they greet each other, they immediately start chatting non-stop.

After the long pleasantries, Sofia tells Cosmo that after a lot of research, she finally discovered what she was looking for. She couldn't believe her luck that Cosmo was the main owner of this law firm, but that this was not the reason she came here. She explains to him that his law firm is involved in the closure of Selvante Industries, a large textile business which employees most of her townsfolk. Without that business, her town will be decimated. She explains there is so much pressure coming from this law firm, because the landlord they represent wants Selvante out, due to unfair increased unpaid rents. The landlord wants to give the government the land to create a potential fracking site. The townsfolk are hardworking and willing people with highly specialised skills and Selvante has been the bedrock of this small town for generations. The business has been trying hard to access funds, but even banks are also unwilling to help as the landlord is a powerful figure. Her husband, a key worker at the Selvante plant, is worried every night about how he will pay the bills along with other workers at the plant, and he is not alone. As an act of desperation, she came here to plead with Cosmo for help and to ask him to do something about this; the townsfolk are desperate. Cosmo diligently takes all the information in that Sofia presents to him.

Cosmo admires Sofia's determination and courage to help her town. But he also remembers the lesson his mum taught and the effect that a town without jobs can have on people's lives. Remembering when he first met Sofia as an angry child, shouting out at being poor, it was his first lesson on Economics 101.

'This, I didn't expect; Sofia, I can't believe it's you.' Cosmo spluttered. 'I had no idea my law firm were involved in this case. Come with me.' The personal assistant takes them back to the boardroom where presentations are still going on. As Cosmo enters the room, presentations stop. Cosmo summons up his most authoritative manner.

'Who is dealing with the Selvante case?' A senior lawyer put his hands up. 'What's your name?' Cosmo asks.

'Leton Greggs, Sir,' he replies.

Cosmo looks directly at him. 'I want you to drop this case, Leton. I know there will be ramifications about this with our existing clients, but it's a conflict of interest. There will be a loss of revenue, I totally understand that, but I need you to drop this case, and do it now.'

There was a cacophony of voices as the senior partners try to reason with Cosmo, trying to convey the long-term impact this move will have and that their major client is a figure not to be messed with. Cosmo listens attentively and starts to panic slightly.

'Have you got a private room I can make a phone call please?' The personal assistant takes Cosmo to one nearby. Back at the boardroom there is a major discussion going on with Sofia about how it is just business, and they are simply representing clients against the Selvante industries. The landlord is a powerful client of this law firm, who brings in a lot of revenue for them. Meanwhile, alone in the private room, Cosmo contacts Lucille via his business card. The business card does a quick self-preservation security scan of the room and Lucille is contacted.

'Lucille, what am I going to do? I want to help Selvante Industries, because for once I am in a position where I can actually help someone. Please tell me what are our options; I know you have been listening. I need your help.'

Lucille sighs in frustration, via the hologram appearing from the business card. 'You just couldn't keep quiet could you? Do you know how much more work for me there is to do? Why, oh why?'

'Just please, help me out will you, Lucille?' pleads Cosmo, speaking quietly.

'Do you know how busy I am? This extra work load will cause backlogs elsewhere, not to mention the resources I'll need to put into it. And I'll need a holiday after this.' Lucille says like a frustrated teenager throwing a tantrum.

Despite Lucille moaning, she does some quick calculations and in a matter of seconds gives a dismissive hand wave. 'Fine, all done. I have listened to your boardroom conversations and made the arrangements with this law firm not to represent the landlord. They should be getting emails now about exactly what to do, with minimum risk involved and also I have given them improvement options to generate maximum revenue that will exceed an over reliance on this landlord client of theirs. For Selvante, I have also made improvement options and will be contacting them on behalf of the Rhinemoore Corporation. They will be fully operational, with the new improvements taking place, in the next couple of weeks. Smart Garments using up to date Graphene technology is the way forward for commercial success. The long-term prospects, after the analysis I have done, which is also in the report being delivered to Selvante, shows positive thirty to forty year projections. I have looked into Selvante's assets and their new specialisation strategy, which is looking very prosperous. With a new recruitment and training drive, which has already been initiated, they will be operating at full capacity for many years to come.'

Cosmo is just nodding his head trying to take in all this information from Lucille.

'What, wait, so it's all done?' Cosmo gasped.

'Yes, all done,' replies Lucille.

'Then why are you having the ultimate tantrum and having a go at me? That was the biggest farzee ever Lucille!! Lucille, you are amazing, I would hug you if I was there. Right, I have to go. Great work, Lucille, you're the best!' Back at Hubris Crux, Lucille can be seen with a shy smile, as she leaves the call.

Cosmo leaves the private room and makes his way to the boardroom. Before he enters, he takes a deep breath and relaxes his mind, which gives him a clarity of thought and a boost of confidence. As he enters the room, there are all sorts of squabbles and discussions taking place. The senior partners ask Cosmo to please reconsider his decision, afraid of what the ramifications will be from their landlord client. Everybody turns around to face Cosmo, they all stop talking.

'Can I have everyone's attention please?' Everyone is paying attention to Cosmo. 'First of all, thank you all for your patience. Any time now you will be getting emails from my team about exactly how to approach the Selvante case, what to do and how I want you to do it. It is not in Rhinemoore's interest to lose revenue and gain bad exposure. But trust me, we have already put a plan in place and have given you options about how to generate further revenue that exceeds an over reliance on certain clients only. There will be no loss of jobs - let's be clear. Sofia, go back to your husband and tell him he can sleep a lot better tonight. We will be handling the Selvante case from now on. We have also put a plan together, which the owners will receive shortly. The future looks good for Selvante; this relationship is just the beginning and you will be the spokesperson for Selvante. I have already made the necessary arrangements. This relationship between Rhinmoore and Selvante is worth more than you can think right now. As for my valued colleagues here, you might tell me about the long-term drawbacks of losing valuable clients etc., or say the landlord is a powerful figure; but believe me when I say, me and my team have forecast models predicting the next forty years of profit, with clear strategies to move forward and precise contingency plans to implement, if necessary. You are all in good hands, I am not worried about a single client who might be upset. So stop this squabbling, read your emails, digest the information, and act upon it now. Then if you have any questions, please contact my team. You, Leton, I expect good things from you, I want you in charge of dealing with Selvante, moving forward.'

Leton looks shocked to be singled out and everyone else in the room is silent and amazed at how quickly Cosmo has responded to deal with this potential crisis. His resolutions have been swift and he shows them solutions so effectively. As Cosmo shakes everyone's hands, he is hugged by Sofia, who cannot contain her relief and newfound optimism. Cosmo leaves the meeting and heads outside, where Tom is waiting for him to take him home. It's been a productive afternoon Cosmo thinks to himself and continues to listen to his music in the car.

As Cosmo and Tom drive home along the long stretched highway, they are suddenly surrounded by four fast approaching SUVs and a helicopter bearing down on them. Tom is forced to stop in the middle of the deserted highway. Armed guards get out of their vehicles and surround their car.

Tom tells Cosmo not to panic, and then suddenly a business executive looking person, tall and slim comes out of the landed helicopter. She makes her way to Cosmo's limousine, standing outside both their car windows.

'My name is Lydia Harris; sorry to bother you, we come in peace; we want to have a chat with Mr Griffin. The landlord wants to meet him to discuss immediate concerning affairs. A few miles north from here, there is a diner, 'Diner46'. Shall we meet in ten minutes?' With the propeller blades still turning, Lydia has struggled to get her voice out.

At a distance, there seems to be a row of cars on the highway now, heading towards the stationary vehicles. 'What do you want to do, Cosmo? This seems serious.' Tom asks, as he looks very concerned.

'Let's go to the meeting,' Cosmo says hesitantly. Tom gives the thumbs up and nods his head in agreement towards Lydia. Everyone vacates to their intended destination. Cosmo's smartphone starts to ring, it is Lucille.

'Don't panic, your bio scan indicates, you are highly stressed and in discomfort. So you are on your way to an unofficial meeting. Leave it to me first to find out some details. Just try to remain calm and find out what they want. I don't know, but perhaps be yourself this time.'

Cosmo interrupts Lucille, 'Lucille, keep calm, calm?! What the hell! I am about to go into a meeting with armed guards and you're telling me, it's going to be fine?' Cosmo says panic stricken.

Lucille with her soft tone, like the sound of his mother replies, 'Rationality leads to intelligent decisions, Cosmo, but being highly emotional leads to irrational decisions. You're going to be fine. There is a high probability they need you alive than dead.' Lucille seems to be getting through to Cosmo, who is a bit more relaxed.

'Lucille, please, be on auto dial when I need you and thanks I needed that pep talk.' Cosmo puts the phone down and thinks rationally, well if they wanted him dead, he probably would be by now.

As they approach the Diner46 carpark, everyone is waiting for them, including Lydia, at the front entrance. Tom parks the car and they both make their way into the diner; night is now starting to fall.

'You don't need to come in with me, Tom, please stay in the car. The meeting is with me.' Cosmo tells Tom nervously.

'Much appreciated, Cosmo, but I won't leave your side. I'm ex-Navy SEAL, Sir.'

As they walk inside the empty diner, they both shake hands with Lydia who escorts both of them to the Landlord, who is sat down at the end of the diner, in a red booth. The Landlord is waiting for them, eating a burger.

'Guys, please take a seat, they do really nice burgers and fries here, who would have thought.' The Landlord seems cheerful with himself.

Both Cosmo and Tom look at each other, and sit down on the opposite side, facing the Landlord.

'Sorry where are my manners, they call me the Landlord. I own most of the major commercial properties and estates on the West Coast. Normally, I would not meet in person and simply let Lydia conduct the meetings on my behalf. But I just had to meet this, Cosmo Griffin, the talk of the town, everyone wants to know you. A myth out of nowhere, who is this guy, the man with the 'Midas touch,' who drives around in a Century Royal limousine? Even I can't get one!' Cosmo has started to blush, red faced. 'You know humans are the only ones on this planet that can actually blush!' the Landlord says confidently. The Landlord is a middle aged man with a stocky build, in a suit wearing sunglasses placed on top of his shaved head.

'So what is this meeting about? I take it you're upset with me, now representing Selvante and that we won't be representing you anymore? Is that correct? By the way, you have a piece of diamond missing on your glasses.' Speaks Cosmo in a relaxed confident manner. Inside he is still wracked with nerves. 'Is Landlord your real name? That's quite a title.'

The Landlord smiles, 'It's actually Ha-yoon Montgomery the Second. Oh will you look at that! You're right, Mr

Griffin, a diamond is missing.' The Landlord gestures to Lydia to take his pair of glasses. She places them delicately in a cloth and takes them away. 'Half a million dollars down the drain. I like perfection, those glasses, are now tainted. Let me get straight to the point, you will keep representing me and leave Selvante alone, to fall and crumble; it's inevitable.'

Cosmo ponders for a few moments, with disdain, the pomposity of this man, 'Half a million dollar glasses? That's just a rich man's first world problems. Moving on, if I oppose what you're recommending, then what?' Cosmo says, shrugging his shoulders.

The Landlord switches from charming to ruthlessness, and in a menacing tone of voice replies, 'Oh sorry, my bad. It isn't a recommendation, it's an order. If you don't do it, then I will personally see to the downfall of the Rhinemoore Corporation. I have connections with the law, politicians you name it, they will be in my pocket and I have dirt on some of the high profile lawyers and partners working for you. I can make life pleasant or unpleasant for you, it's as simple as that.' The landlord says in a firm way, slurping on his soft drink casually. Cosmo is stunned, he has never been threatened like this before, but at the same time this is no longer the same Cosmo either.

'It seems you really haven't given me any options; yet, a meeting is based on negotiations?' Cosmo says looking directly at the Landlord with intent.

In the meantime, some of the senior armed guards are talking to Lydia, 'This is the first time I have seen the Landlord come out on short notice. This guy must be important.'

'The Landlord wants to establish if Cosmo can be bought or leveraged. This guy has no history, but to be that savvy with his investments... I've never seen it before,' Lydia says talking quietly, looking quite impressed with Cosmo.

'It's the other guy you need to be worried about immediately. That's Mr Greenman, decorated soldier of the past, a fighter you don't want lingering around in this meeting.' Lydia orders the armed guards to get in position, to be ready, just in case.

Just then a waitress comes over with two burger and fries, with two soft drinks, for Cosmo and Tom.

'I'm just going to go to the men's room and think about what you're proposing.' Cosmo gets up and makes his way to the men's room, surprisingly he is not followed. Sitting in a cubicle, he contacts Lucille, 'Anything, Lucille? What do you have?'

Lucille talks discreetly via his business card, 'You have several options at your disposal right now. We can deplete the Landlord's assets in a number of minutes, rendering all his financial status worthless, although the knock-on effect to innocent people will be severe financially. Next option, we can tell him to do his best through the courts, although the immediate risk of danger to your life does increase to seventy percent, so I wouldn't recommend that option. We can use the vaporisation option, which is the most viable option you have and means everything is taken care of in a matter of minutes. It will take me a couple minutes to organise, but the outcome long-term seems to lead to minimal complications and least impediment to hinder Rhinemoore's progress. If you can confirm which level of vaporisation option you would prefer, I can start to initiate proceedings, just let me know time scales. Interestingly, Tej has found that there is a link to your past, maybe you want to utilise this and also the medical records, which he has accessed. Worthless information, of no relevance if you ask me.'

Meanwhile, back at the red booth, Tom tries to reason with the Landlord. 'Is this all necessary, Cosmo is a good man trying to do the right thing. Is this an ego trip? No one has confronted you before? I've seen and worked with men like you before, soon or later all sins catch up to us. Schadenfreude.' Tom says in a calm manner.

'I'm not that bad once you get to know me, really. A wise person told me once 'A widower only knows a widow's sorrow!', I don't do sorrow. They all cower before me eventually, not impressed with your boss who has gone to the toilet. Please eat your burger, seriously, it's going to get cold.' The Landlord totally dismisses Tom's plea. Tom should be shocked, but isn't surprised with the Landlord's response and looks around for options, discreetly checking out his local vicinity.

Moments later, Cosmo leaves the men's room, takes a deep breath and sits down in the red booth. 'Right, Ha-yoon, in about 10 minutes you are going to have an epiphany. So, I give you two options! First option is walk away, enjoy life and stop threatening people. Second option, wait for 10 minutes' because my answer is still the same. Rhinemoore bows to no one and you might have leverage over some of my employees, but that does not scare me. We will keep representing Selvante and that's final. Guys, can we all just enjoy our burgers. Come on, Tom eat up.'

All of a sudden, the Landlord is a bit apprehensive as he continues eating his burger, wondering to himself. *Why hasn't Cosmo flinched, is he bluffing? Who is this person to defy me? Have I not been clear, does he not know the gravitas of the situation?* The Landlord wasn't expecting a reaction like this, as he is so used to people folding, bowing and cowering in front of him.

'Come on, Tom eat up. Ha-yoon is right, this burger is delicious, sweet potato fries for the win. On a side note, Ha-yoon, I'm looking around, and what do your henchmen do, when they are not with you? Do they go on vacations, have fun, spend time with family?' Cosmo says in an upbeat, curious manner. All three are eating together, with Tom eating cautiously. It's been over ten minutes. Eventually, after a few more minutes, they have finished their burgers wiping their mouths and hands.

'Don't worry about my henchmen, they are more like a means to an end, getting paid to carry out specific functions upon my request. Tell me, Cosmo, you haven't flinched once or got worried about who I am. How do you think this meeting will end, Cosmo Griffin? How do think this meeting will turn out, in your eyes? There are no positive outcomes for you and your driver in any scenario I can see.'

Cosmo looks directly at the Landlord, 'Arrogance is the birth child of ignorance! You can't see, because you're looking at the wrong scenario!' The Landlord is stunned into silence, as Cosmo continues, 'I'm confident and happy you will do the right thing and that's the truth. Also, what does family mean to you?'

The Landlord starts laughing furiously, 'What a guy! Seriously, that's your answer? Family is everything. But when people enter my territory without my permission or know how, there is only one outcome.'

'Oh cool, like you invading my territory on the highway?' Cosmo looks at him with a raised eyebrow, 'What good are you to the family, if you can't look after yourself? Your health is important, what's your legacy? I know everything about you, Ha-yoon, your family history, your health, your bowel movements? Shall I carry on?' Cosmo asks again, but this time full of confidence. The Landlord is stunned by his line of questioning; he is silent for a few minutes tongue-tied pondering on an answer. There is a slight sheen of sweat from the Landlord's forehead making its way down his face. Cosmo gives him a serviette, implying to wipe the sweat from his face.

Moments later, there are bright lights over the diner, coming from the sky. Lydia and the armed guards go outside, to investigate. The Landlord jumps out of his seat, clearly rattled, trying to find out what is going on.

Cosmo, in the meantime, is slurping on his soft drink. 'You know I hate these new paper straws, they are the worst thing. Please sit down, you are stressing yourself out, think about your health.' Tom is looking at Cosmo confused, but in total admiration of his confidence in standing up to this tyrant. He thinks to himself, *could this be the ruthlessness coming out of Cosmo, that's he's heard so much about. Maybe he has underestimated Cosmo too?*

Suddenly the entrance door is swung open. A gentleman is ushered towards the three still sat at the red booth. It is the old, angry owner of the Korean restaurant. Cosmo tells the owner that Ha-yoon is his illegitimate son, the son he abandoned many years ago.

The Landlord gasps, 'What is going on, is this a joke?' He is in denial, anger and frustration are all emotions going through Ha-yoon's perplexed mind, visible for everyone to see.

'Nope, Ha-yoon. He is your real father. Here is your proof,' Cosmo says as the old angry Korean owner hands him a piece of paper with all the information on it. Both parent and son are gobsmacked, they don't know what to say.

'I will let you both catch up on lost time, remember Ha-yoon, you can't buy time back, this is one purchase you cannot afford' Cosmo pats the old angry Korean guy on the shoulder, reassuring him.

Cosmo and Tom then stand up and make their way to the diner counter to get more drinks and give the pair of them space for reconciliation. Both parent and son sit down, shouting, screaming, tears in their eyes can be seen.

'What on earth is going on?' Tom asks curiously, as everything spoken between them is in Korean.

'Long story short, 'old angry Korean guy', who I used to pot wash for as a teen, has been angry ever since I can remember. He's been angry ever since he found out his lover at the time ran away with another bloke whilst she was pregnant with his baby. He had no idea she was cheating. From what I am hearing, she was the love of his life, but he was never good enough for her family and always paranoid with their wealth. I found out that the old angry Korean guy was searching for his girlfriend and unborn child all these years. Every time his quest fell short. I presume it was because of her family interfering.

So, I arranged a helicopter to pick him up when I found out the link between him and Ha-yoon. I'm hoping he lets Selvante go, I do have back up plans to back up plans, just in case.' Cosmo chuckles to himself.

Tom looks dumbfounded, 'You know what, Cosmo I have never met a guy quite like you before, seriously.' Tom, cheers to his soft drink.

'Thanks, Tom as my mom would say, the easy choice is always the fake option, whereas the hard choices in life is always the real option. By the way thanks for having my back. So, ex-Navy SEAL? Wow, that is awesome.' Cosmo cheers with his soft drink.

The screams and shouting have subsided with parent and son crying, rejoicing and hugging each other. The Landlord comes over to Cosmo and pats him on the back. 'Cosmo, Cosmo, Cosmo, what am I going to do with you? For the first time in my life I have been impressed, somehow you managed to pull this off. How is anyone's guess? I am speechless. You know what? I am going to give

Selvante a pass. Hell, they can have the land too. I'll get Lydia onto it ASAP. But, I do want to have a working relationship with Rhinemoore Corporation, specifically you, Cosmo. Help me change, what do you think?'

Cosmo puts one hand on Ha-yoon's shoulder, 'So you want to change? I suggest, change your life, change your circle of friends. Only you can make that choice. Take your parents' financial status away. Ha-yoon, what kind of man are you? Can you really stand on your own two feet? In the end it boils down to... what have you done without any help or assistance, that you can say, you're truly proud of. I think we can work something out, so let's toast to a new partnership with a round of soft drinks.' Cosmo says looking very satisfied with himself.

Ha-yoon with a beaming smile, laughs. 'This guy, this guy is out of this world, the Midas myth is true.' He says to Tom.

Ha-yoon's father comes across and gives Cosmo the biggest hug ever, almost squeezing the life out of him. For the first time, he says, in broken English, 'You can know a promising tree from when it's a baby tree, I have watched you grow up. You, Cosmo, I will always be grateful to, for the gift you have given me tonight. All those lost years, wondering, thank you. Twenty percent off to you and your family in my restaurant any time.' He says jokingly.

Cosmo smiles says, 'Any time, guys.' He shakes their hands and says his goodbyes. As they leave the front entrance, Lydia greets them.

'I have never seen Ha-yoon laugh like that before, it's impressive. I don't know who you are, Cosmo Griffin, but I would like to find out. Here's my business card, call me some time.' Lydia's last sentence, she speaks seductively.

'Erm thanks, don't know what to say.' Cosmo seems surprised.

Both Cosmo and Tom make their way back to the car. 'Never a dull moment with you, Cosmo!' Tom opens the door and smiles to himself.

Back at Hub City, Lucille is showing Tej around, 'I just need to check in on Cosmo, to make sure that he is doing as he is told. I have not heard from him in a while.' Her holographic image beams from her chest with calculations and formulas being presented. 'As well as rearranging paternity papers there's logistics to sort now. Damn it, Cosmo! He should have activated the vaporisation option instead, by far the most efficient way to solve this problem. But does he ever listen to me? No! Why are primitives so annoying and complex? This Landlord might cause problems later on for Cosmo statistically speaking.'

Tej looks at Lucille, 'Vaporising certain chemicals and blood vessels to cause a mild heart attack in the Landlord's body, is not really Cosmo's style, but underestimate Cosmo at your peril.'

'These primitives are so unpredictable; I will have to recalibrate my contingency settings.' Lucille looks angry and frustrated again. AIs in general cannot understand the value of life overall and the complex relationships different species have between them. They can't see beyond the relationship they have with their immediate species, who they work with.

AIs do not really appreciate that species have a finite life span. Tej, on the other hand, seems to understand this and appreciates even more the value of life. Although, he cannot understand the full extent of this, because his memory and data is in parts, some being lost for an unknown reason. There is a big difference between new and old tech AIs and the interaction they have between species.

Tej smiles, 'Admit it, you are starting to care for Cosmo? You need to see the real beauty of life; it will blow your mind. Complexities exist in formulas and calculations, but the formations are endless in the real world. Cosmo is awesome. Oh look, Lucille, let's pretend to join the protest at city square.' Lucille does a face palm and is dragged by Tej towards the protests.

'We still have to ask the senior AIs why Cosmo can see Alluca in her primitive form? But this is quite fun too.' Lucille grabs a placard, 'We want AI rights; we want individual names!' Shouts Lucille really enjoying herself. Tej looks in dismay, thinking Lucille already has a name. She is not known as a number anymore and chuckles to himself, but he also plays along in the protest. Both AIs are having fun, something Lucille has not experienced before. This is the first AI friend that Lucille has had, she likes the fact that Tej has a unique perspective on life and always has fun, albeit often with annoying timing.

As they both leave the protests, they are approached by other AIs who recognise her and are ecstatic to meet Lucille. They want to know what it is like to work for a primitive.

'You're working with that primitive, aren't you L23UC1ll310?' Asks one AI.

'Is it true they make you do a lot of work?'

For AIs the greatest thrill is getting work to do and research to undertake; the more work AIs get, the greater the thrill and experience for them.

Lucille looks annoyed, 'First of all, that primitive is known as Cosmo.' The other AIs look stunned. 'And secondly, I'm the one looking after him most of the time and my name is Lucille.'

The AIs are totally shocked at the thought, as AIs refer to the species they work with as superiors.

'You're so lucky your superior gives you a lot of work to do.'

Another AI pipes up, 'I cannot believe you have a name, my superior will never allow it, nevermind me calling her by her name. You must be the first AI I have ever met like this; it is an absolute honour meeting you.'

Lucille ponders on that response, maybe she is quite lucky to be working with Cosmo and should appreciate him for all his faults and positives.

Other AIs are looking at Tej in a peculiar manner, 'You are weird looking, why?'

Tej is just about to speak when Lucille interrupts, 'Whether he looks weird or not, it is not really your concern. I mean your face and that body doesn't really go together does it? Let's go, Tej.'

Other AIs can be seen giggling in the background. 'She is my hero!' One AI can be heard saying, in full admiration of Lucille. Tej is surprised with a beaming face full of pride, from Lucille's reaction. He notices she is learning certain traits from Cosmo and doesn't realise it yet.

'Let's go and meet the senior AIs, and see if they can help us with our query.' As Lucille drags Tej away, the other curious AIs are looking at him.

Back on CX321, sat in his limousine, Cosmo reflects upon his last three days. He is quite happy with himself, how he handled this situation with Selvante. Things look quite optimistic, as he looks forward to his challenging new life.

Tom, as usual, puts some nice progressive house tunes for Cosmo to relax to, as they drive home. Cosmo is shattered as he enters his parent's apartment. He greets his parents, who are watching TV, and goes straight to his bedroom.

'What an eventful few days it has been, hopefully tomorrow will be a lot easier. How stressful can an induction day be?' He says out loud. Later on the evening, his mom checks up on him to see if he is okay or wants anything to eat, but Cosmo is in bed fast asleep.

She looks at Glen, 'You know, Glen, this is the first time I can feel good things will happen for our boy. Can you imagine he and Jenny getting together, the kids?'

'Oh Lord. Hun just give it a rest; I know you're excited, but geez, just let the boy do his own thing.'

Cosmo's mom has a tear in her eye, 'I know, but he will always be our Cossy. I saw the disappointment on his face, time and time again growing up, wanting to go out, be with friends, go and party. But instead he was looking after you. His whole childhood was making sure we were okay, taking responsibility and he never once complained.'

Glen walks to her and gives her a hug, 'Well he did have that major farzee when he was ten, remember? When you had taken him to some charity soup kitchen.' At first Jasmine seems puzzled, but then she remembers with glee.

'You know I totally forgot about that, I doubt Cossy still remembers that. I just want him to be happy and be successful in life and marry Jenny. Then when they have kids, I can take care of the grandchildren. Is that too much to ask?'

Glen rolls his eyes and hugs her more affectionately. 'And all I want is for your mom to stop being annoying. Now that Cosmo has a good job, we can give her a call and rub it in!' Jasmine stops hugging Glen and punches him on the shoulder. 'Ouch!'

Chapter 8 ¬ The Impossible Case

In the middle of the night, Alluca uses the Jauntewarpe to travel to Cosmo's bedroom.

'Wake up primitive! Wake up, Cosmo! You are on the clock.' She says, as Cosmo wakes up grudgingly, still dazed after being suddenly awoken from a deep sleep, slobbering on his pillow.

'Be quiet, your parents are asleep. I have taken the liberty of writing them a note to say that you had to leave early for a case.' Alluca speaks quietly.

'Do you always have to pick me up when I'm passed out? What's the rush? It's only an induction day.' Cosmo says half asleep. Alluca then snatches the duvet off him and to her surprise, Cosmo is just in his boxer shorts. She quickly looks at her business card awkwardly. Whilst Cosmo is getting dressed, she notices Cosmo's full body and gets distracted.

'Hurry up, Cosmo. Are you done getting dressed? Your species is weird and disgusting,' she mutters.

'Oh really? Says the three-legged freak with two brains,' Cosmo retorts. 'Right, ready. Where do you want my thumb print?' Just like that with a single press of a thumb, the Jauntewarpe portal opens up and takes both of them away immediately. 'So what is the big deal, why so early? Don't you Zargboyans need sleep too?' Asks Cosmo.

'We sleep every forty-eight hours, according to your primitive timing, and part of me can switch off completely, while the other side of me works through,' replies Alluca.

'That's erm, awesome and incredible! You see you do have super powers, wow I wasn't expecting that.' Cosmo says in admiration.

Every time Cosmo is near Alluca he is drawn to her and cannot stop from falling for her a little bit more each time they interact, he still hasn't figured out a way to ask her on a date yet. He knows there is no chance with her, as she is so high up there and respected like a superior master, a super star throughout the galaxy. Plus, to her, primitives are disgusting. But Cosmo will still keep trying to woo her, even though it is an 'impossible case.' For Cosmo it is a deeper attraction then just physical but he can't explain it.

As they arrive at the Hubris Crux, 'So remember when your name went up on the large view terminal screen? Well, that's what I was enquiring about, it is not an induction, I wish it was. Someone else was in charge of that case but, for unforeseen reasons, you have been chosen to lead it instead and my seniors want you to represent this case against the Tarn Corporation. The case date has been moved up to the Intergalactic Court of Omens. Now there are various levels of courts, but you just landed the big one. You have roughly two hours before court proceedings start. It's an impossible case. No one has ever won it, though many have tried, so there is no pressure to succeed. Just remember it will be broadcast to the entire ten sectors, so do not do anything to put KillaRhinepor's name in disrepute. In other words, don't do anything stupid. We want to increase our positive image rankings for KillaRhinepor. You are expected to lose this case; just make a good showing of yourself, that's all we want. Lucille and Tej will give you an update with the case files and proceedings. Your first clients are Mr and Mrs BukseriyaBal, of the Gauwladykes species.'

'Wow. That's a lot to take in. I will do my best representing this corporation, I guess. What's the worst that can happen? My first client how exciting.' Cosmo replies as calmly as possible, but his heart is beating faster. 'So much for it not being a stressful day!' He mutters to himself. Cosmo is being thrown in at the deep end and the only problem is? There is no bottom. All Cosmo's experiences to date, both professionally and personally, have come down to this moment. *But I've just saved my planet from destruction, so surely this is going to be a piece of cake. And the Landlord, look how I dealt with that situation.* He thinks to himself.

As Cosmo steps into his blends, the whole office has entirely changed to accommodate the Gauwladykes' personality, which is one of nature; a log cabin kind of feel, blended with wooden technology complexities of various holographic household gadgets on the walls. This effect is to make them feel at ease and show respect. Cosmo takes a deep breath the reality hits him, they are his first clients, who happen to be aliens.

The Gauwladykes, who are sat down on the couch, are like the cutest giant teddy bear species around. Six feet tall, both covered in silky pink fur, but smartly dressed and with razor sharp teeth. Lucille hands Cosmo the case files by transferring data onto his business card, with some abbreviated notes and gives the Gauwladykes both a hot drink and native snacks.

Suddenly Tej blurts out, 'Hi, I'm Tej. It is a pleasure to meet you. My history data has found a few interesting unique links between the Gauwladykes species and the human species, Sir.' Tej speaks emphatically to Cosmo.

'Really, I'm intrigued.' Cosmo replies.

'Well for starters, Mr BukseriyaBal, your great Gauwladyke explorer Mr RoonAsh, actually crash landed on your planet, Cosmo by mistake well over a century ago. In the northern parts of America, Mr RoonAsh inadvertently created the Bigfoot mythos when he was spotted by a local hunter. Mr RoonAsh also had a run in with a famous toy maker whose son had spotted him, thus creating the first teddy bear design, eventually naming it after the famous leader of America. The late Mr RoonAsh managed to escape your planet after spending half a century trapped there until the technology was developed enough. Interestingly, he brought back seeds of the redwood part of the coniferous tree family. Which was extinct on the Gauwladyke planet, but now after plantation the redwood thrives and is a core material with electricity conductive elements, once liquid is added to it. All because of Mr RoonAsh's unintended voyage. It is also the same material on your pendant, Mr BukeriyaBal.' Tej seems very proud of himself.

'Wow, that is amazing, Tej. Erm I guess, thanks for sharing that information.' Cosmo looks a bit confused.

'It was an ice breaker for you, Sir.' Tej whispers to Cosmo and gives him a cheeky wink.

Cosmo acknowledges Tej and gets back to his files. He is scanning, going through the case notes via holographic images emanating from his business card. He then turns to the Gauwladykes, 'Hi, I'm Cosmo Griffin nice to meet you guys.' Cosmo shakes both of their hands. 'Okay, so here it says your species were all made redundant from the Tarn Corporation with no severance package.'

'Yes and we said it was fine,' Mr BukseriyaBal says calmly in a deep voice.

'But, why?' Cosmo says looking confused and perplexed.

'Because that's what we do. It is our way, our beliefs.' Mrs BukseriyaBal explains.

Cosmo looks more puzzled and asks, 'Let me guess you have to say yes or agree to everything? Surely not! I mean that would be a little crazy, right?'

'No, not everything that would be weird.' Both husband and wife chuckle to themselves. 'Being polite and saying yes is our way of life, we believe it is fundamental to our species' survival and because of this we have thrived.'

'Oh boy! But you do know the Tarn Corporation has taken your wages and future income for your loved ones and future generations, and given you no compensation at all for your entire species? You think that is right or fair? You are happy with this?' Cosmo asks in astonishment.

'Yes. Why are we here again? They keep sending us to courts, but the Tarn Corporation has been good to us, so what is the problem?' Mrs BukseriyaBal shrugs while Alluca face palms.

Cosmo tries again. 'You are here to help put a wrong right, but importantly, to help future Gauwladykes prosper and succeed in life. To not let them take your assets, your life's work. Erm, Alluca, there are weird numbers for me that don't make sense in the file. What and how much are they owed in primitive monetary value?'

Alluca does some calculations on her business card. 'Monetary and assets combined you mean? Let me work it out...that is roughly $960 trillion dollars.'

'Sorry what did you say? Oh my god, $960 trillion dollars!' Cosmo's mouth falls open, as he finds himself pacing up and down with his hands on his hips and then clutching his head in a nervous sweat.

'This primitive seems stressed, would you like a cup of hot gauwlesso?' Mrs BukseriyaBal comes over to Cosmo and pats him on the shoulder. Alluca chuckles.

'Thank you, I'm fine.' Cosmo re-adjusts his tie and composure before turning his attention to Alluca. 'I see you gave me this case because it is impossible for them to say no. It's like a test is it? God damn it.' Cosmo drags his hand down his face. 'Oh Lord help me. Alluca can you not zap their brains or use mental powers on them?' He says, in a discreet manner to Alluca.

Turning back to his clients, he says, 'So, to clarify: you cannot say no when it comes to professionalism? The Tarn Corporation knows this and in court they will have a field day just because you say yes to everything.'

Alluca intervenes as the Gauwladykes look confused. 'Yes, pretty much,' she shrugs. 'By the way, court proceedings are in one hour. Don't worry, Cosmo, this case has been to court countless times and it's never been won. Your two AIs will assist you with everything you need. I need to go to another meeting, but good luck on your first galactic court appearance.' Alluca smiles and leaves the office.

'Right, I shall see you, Mr and Mrs BukseriyaBal, in an hour. We have lots to work on. It's been emotional, thank you.' Cosmo says to the two teddy bear aliens.

'Oh how delightful. Yes, of course. Every time we have been to court it doesn't seem to last very long, no matter how hard you lawyers try. So, please don't stress yourself out too much, Mr Griffin. It will be fine, do not forget to smile, say yes and be respectfully polite.' Mrs BukseriyaBal pats him on the back again.

As the Gauwladykes leave, Cosmo is pacing up and down his office, trying to think of a strategy. 'Right, Tej. Can you please find all the history you can on the heritage of the Gauwladykes? I can't see any on the case files? And Lucille, please find out as much as you can about the history of the Tarn Corporation and the links they have with the Gauwladykes. Is there any connection that has been missed, even if it is insignificant? I need to find out! How did the Gauwladykes come to be? Are kids born saying yes? Why does this happen, how does this happen? I have not got time to look through all the files Come on guys what is the real connection with the Tarn corporation, go, go, go!'

As Lucille and Tej start their searches, anything of relevance is transferred in bullet points to Cosmo's business card.

'Do we have a pen and paper, so I can start plotting a strategy,' he asks. Lucille arranges something better, an interactive white board which appears on the wall. 'That's awesome, Lucille, right let's get started. That's interesting, Tej, weird initiation ceremony. Hmm interesting, go deeper on that aspect, Tej. I might have an angle on this case, it's worth a shot.'

'Shall I put on some progressive house music, Sir? Help sharpen your concentration and focus.' Tej says knowing time is of the essence.

'You read my mind, Tej, thanks.' Cosmo says frantically whilst trying to ascertain a motive.

Lucille is confused with Tej's advice, but is side tracked, impressed with Cosmo's thinking. Lucille gets on board and also shows more enthusiasm to help Cosmo, who is now using his dad's ER's theory displayed on the interactive white board. It seems that what Cosmo is thinking and muttering is visibly seen on the screen automatically, just like Cosmo would do, if he was scribbling on a piece of paper with arrows, diagrams everywhere. For the first time, all three are working as a team, working on theories, strategies, looking at the options they have available. Cosmo is trying to develop back up plans, to back up plans, trying to work out the opposition strategy.

Meanwhile, Alluca is having chats with her superiors including Marfa, although it is more of a disagreement. 'Is this really fair on Cosmo, his first case is the Gauwladykes? It's a lot of pressure, even I would be hesitant to take this case on and against Mr Annoose of all lawyers too. It's pretty obvious the Tarn Corporation wants to undermine us, in front of every sector to show their strength and gain more market share.'

Alluca's senior, an older and wiser Zargboyan male, Marfa listens to her worries. 'I understand your hesitancy, however like you said before it's an impossible case, we are not worried about winning this case because you can't. We know this, everyone knows this. But the positive exposure Cosmo will give us and this corporation will be beneficial. For some reason, Cosmo is resonating with all species like we have never seen before. There is logic in play, not the logic you will agree with and I understand your hesitation about that.' Alluca still shakes her head in disagreement.

During the Jauntewarpe journey to the court, both Lucille and Tej have been filling Cosmo in on the formalities of court proceedings. Cosmo seems like he has a strategy and plays out the proceedings in his mind, occasionally muttering to himself going into his 'Clarity of Thought' mode for a moment, to conjure up some confidence and inspiration. Lucille looks worried.

'Don't worry, Lucille. Sir does this all the time.' Says Tej. Lucille gives Tej a raised eye brow, with a confused look.

'Who am I kidding, I can't do this. This is too much!' Cosmo blurts out.

Just then Tej grabs hold of Cosmo's arm, 'You got this. Like your dad used to say, what's the worst that can happen? Repeat it after me, Sir.' Cosmo and Tej both talk at the same time, 'Keep climbing higher. Serenity is just around the corner.' Tej smiles at Cosmo.

'You're right, Tej, just last minute nerves. It's the anticipation, like a mental pain barrier, putting your mind through the threshold. I've been doing a lot of that lately, I guess I have to overcome this too. It just so happens to be on a galactic scale, but what's the worst that can happen right?' Cosmo says jokingly, who is trembling with nerves and hesitation inside. Cosmo closes his eyes and goes back into his thought process. Lucille, now looking really worried, does a quick bio scan indicating all vital signs are normal, nothing to worry about. She looks at Tej and Cosmo wondering about the dynamics of their relationship, again confused.

Chapter 9 ¬ The Intergalactic Court of Omens

Cosmo and his AIs Jauntewarpe to the Intergalactic Court of Omens via his business card. He is amazed with the number of different species that are already waiting for the case to proceed. Cosmo is standing with his AIs and they are ushered into the courtroom by two creatures that look similar to the Zargboyans, but different. They have much smaller heads with a diamond halo levitating above and they are covered in long purple and yellow gowns. As they enter the courtroom, there is a band playing, a species that looks like the coolest, bright red penguins he has ever seen. They are singing an operatic dance rock ballad to the crowds, all five members are giving it their best to whip the crowds into a frenzy of excitement. There are special hologram effects everywhere, including pyrotechnics and fireworks which touch the crowds' senses. The crowd are in hysteria, clapping, shouting, whistling, and rejoicing. As Cosmo looks around there must be thousands of species packed into this courtroom. He sees various banners and posters, one in particular that catches his eye, is of Alluca: 'We love you Alluca, we love your show, you are the best judge ever.' The atmosphere feels like a gladiatorial arena, however, there it is not gladiators, but lawyers fighting to win a case through intellect and wit.

Cosmo sees the biggest screen he has ever seen, situated behind the main judge, everything is being broadcast live. The main judge is called the Grand Vix Supreme, a yellow octopus - like alien with ten long arms, white hair and a green beard. He also has a halo levitating above his head; a large diamond-shaped ruby, almost like another eye but with independent movement. He looks like an aging hippie or rock star and as he deliberates on event proceedings, he talks like a hippie too. He is also doing his best to gee up the crowds with his flamboyant tantric dance arm movements in tandem with the music.

The court itself is huge and reminds Cosmo of a cross between a theatre and a boxing ring. There are independent lights beaming from above, hovering lights and independent cameras all over, capturing everything. There is different species reporting commentating on the events taking place, in a variety of languages. According to the big screen, Cosmo's case is not even the main event. This probably reflects that the odds of winning this case are very low, impossible even and everyone knows what the outcome will be. His court case is first to proceed; it is at the bottom of a top ten ranking list displayed on the big screen. Different species of all kinds are sitting and watching this with their alien popcorns and drinks by their side, almost like a main sports event, full of anticipation and excitement.

The Gauwladykes are sitting near the front, the best seats in the courtroom, apart from Mr and Mrs BukseriyaBal, who are in special seats ready for questioning. As Cosmo takes his seat with his two AIs, he closes his eyes trying to zone out the atmosphere. He starts to remember his childhood and how he felt shy in large crowds. But for some reason, this feels different, he is actually at peace and feels more at home than ever before. He has overcome the anticipation. Cosmo is not fazed by the whole spectacle, but in actual fact was embracing it. He felt he wasn't that loser, ridiculed as a teenager or the shy kid anymore. He had his parents' love through thick and thin and it didn't matter if he lost this case, he didn't have anything to lose. He only had to prove to himself that he belongs here and that he can give it his best. Cosmo thinks to himself, how his life has changed so much from the moment he made that choice to say yes to adventure with Alluca, when she was sat in his apartment. He has no regrets. It was a choice that makes him now feel like he is standing on the shoulders of destiny.

Finally, the Grand Vix Supreme deliberates on the proceedings, on the Gauwladykes case with hovering speakers broadcasting his voice inside and outside the court. He explains, 'Each lawyer has five times to come up to the main stage and make their main points. In effect, five rounds each, plus a closing final statement from either lawyer. After that, the grand supreme jury will have their say and give their final verdict on the outcome.'

With his eyes still closed, Cosmo is going through his strategy and delivery, muttering to himself about wishers, thinkers, deciders and doers, as he practises the formalities in his head. Across the court, the representatives of the Tarn Corporation are doing the same thing, thirteen of them altogether, various species, sitting behind the main lawyer.

The main lawyer, Mr Annoose, looks like, what can only be described as a four feet tall foetus, with an umbilical cord acting like a third hand known as his kufi. He is dressed in a ruby encrusted suit, which is his trademark look. His face is quite slimy with a mixture of sweat and a pink ooze coming out from top of his head and down his face. The ooze is being collected by some sort of small dog collar around his neck and being recycled through the holes in his neck. His legs are not to be seen, but he instead seems to hover on a green gas cloud. The crowd are sat. There are various banners and posters from different species of certain famous lawyers, showing their full support like real fans do in sports. The four elite lawyers are sat together on a floating couch high above everyone else watching, observing the spectacle. They salute Mr Annoose with conviction as he is part of their niche club.

The words 'Mr Annoose v Mr Griffin, Tarn Corporation v Gauwladykes. Case 23232425', appears on the large screen with Mr Annoose's trademark slogan: 'Winners show no mercy, see me dance, you've lost already.' There is no slogan appearing for Cosmo.

The Grand Vix Supreme is also acting like a boxing ring announcer when two boxers are about to fight and introduces both the lawyers. With great voice projection and a thunderous roar, he says to the crowds, 'The one on the left… the hall of famer, who is with the elites of the elites, immortalised for generations to come, undefeated, he oozes confidence like no other, his legacy is beyond comprehension. The Jengu, the myth, the legend… I give you Mr Annooooooooose.'

The crowd are hysterical shouting, screaming his name, the noise is deafening. Then a few moments later, when the crowd go quiet again, he says, 'And on the right side, a newbie who had his first win on his planet's negotiation contract over the fearsome Queen of Zargboyans, Alluca. We know him as the primitive. Will he live up to that reputation or surprise us, probably not? He looks weird, smells weird, I give yoooou, Mr Griffin!' Again the crowd go wild, but the noise is far below the support for Mr Annoose; the bias is clear for everyone to see.

As the crowd slowly quietens, Mr Annoose can be seen waving to the crowds to calm them down, like a real pro. It is clear he has done this before plenty of times. A charismatic and confident person, beaming for everyone to see, he comes up to the main stage, ready to interrogate Mr and Mrs BukseriyaBal. In her excitement, Mrs BukseriyaBal asks for Mr Annoose's autograph. She holds up her card and Mr Annoose transfers a moving image of himself, with various product endorsements, doing a cheesy pose onto her card. They both say hello to Mr Annoose as they are big fans of his. Seems like everything is against Cosmo at the moment, all the momentum is with Mr Annoose; the crowd, the Gauwladykes, the judge all seem to be in awe of this little lawyer.

Mr Annoose looks at the crowd and jury again. Then with spectacular voice projection, especially for such a small species, he speaks. It is quite magnificent to see, along with his umbilical cord, which is waving at the crowd for enhanced effect. He says, 'My fellow species of all kinds, enjoy the show.' Mr Annoose takes a bow, as you would do for royalty. 'Now I ask, why do we have to put the poor Gauwladykes through this, every time? The KillaRihinepor should be ashamed of themselves, this poor couple.' The crowd are shouting, booing, there are boos all over the court. He continues to talk to the audience, 'They have now given a primitive, yes a primitive, the reins to handle this case. I mean really, how low can this corporation go? This corporation is a glutton for punishment. Loss after loss. Who is in charge of these lawyers, the decision making? Marfa, where are you? I used to respect you as a credible lawyer, are you here? The lawyer once feared throughout the sectors is going senile, just like the corporation he represents. This poor primitive has even given his AIs pet names; AI's have name now? What is that all about? I tell you what. What does the KillaRhinepor Corporation and the intergalactic banks out in sector ten have in common? They both keep losing interest!' The crowd are in hysterics, they are loving the mockery and jibes inflicted upon KillaRhinepor by Mr Annoose. Mr Annoose takes a well-timed, subtle moment to endorse a business. 'I mean have you seen their declining market share results? When will they ever learn? All species want is a corporation that shows the upmost integrity and most of all, a corporation that delivers on their promises, just like the Tarn Corporation does. They deliver and will always delver on their guaranteed pledge, you can take that to the bank. That reminds me, right now out in sector nine, the Bank of Bauti & Zam pride themselves on ten percent interest on savings.' Mr Annoose makes a cheeky smile and does a hand gesture to the main cameras. Every time Mr Annoose makes a comment, there are all sorts of firework images with an arcade retro animation displayed on the big screen. Every point he makes is emphasised more on the big screen to elevate the sheer conviction of his points for everyone to see and heighten their senses.

He then turns to Cosmo and looks at him directly, shaking his head. 'Oh primitive, oh primitive. To give you a case like this of such epic proportions it is so disrespectful to the Gauwladykes. I don't know what to say, I feel embarrassed for you, to be here, defending this, please have some self-respect and go back to CX321. It's fine really, I will pay for your travel ticket personally, so you can get back to enjoying life and whatever it is that primitives love doing. You see, at the Tarn Corporation, we care for species like you, we do the thinking for you!' Crowds are nodding their heads in agreement, as Mr Annoose flamboyantly raises his arms and umbilical cord. He starts doing his trademark robotic shuffle dance as if to insinuate, he has already won this case. The crowd cannot get enough of this entertainment, Mr Annoose then quietens them again and turns his attention towards Mr and Mrs BukseriyaBal.

'So, I have one question only: did you Mr and Mrs BukseriyaBal give permission for the Tarn Corporation to take everything from you in the most amicable way possible? Did you not agree to no severance and no assets left on your planet?' Mr Annoose then turns around to the crowd and raises his arms. The crowd are raising the roof with so much noise. After the noise dissipates, by Mr Annoose calming the crowd down, he gestures to Mr and Mrs BukseriyaBal to respond.

'Ooh, ooh, I can answer that!' Mr BukseryiaBal excitingly stands up. 'Yes, as a collective, we all said yes and agreed to this. The Tarn Corporation has been very good to us for generations, they can take all of our assets, we couldn't accept any compensation, it would be very rude to do so.' The crowd go wild with banners going up saying, 'Go Mr Annoose, go.'

The four elite lawyers sat on their hovering couch can be seen clapping with respect. The big screen is showing a large scale, with a pendulum swinging gaging which way the momentum is going for either Lawyer. The pendulum has totally shifted towards the left side indicating Mr Annoose's victory, so far is inevitable.

'No further questions, your Grand Vix Supreme!' Mr Annoose winks and gives a pointy finger gun gesture to the judge in an overly confident manner. He winks at the crowd, waving his hands like a politician does during a campaign. As he hovers away, Mr Annoose mumbles to himself, 'I can't believe they got me out for this again, why bother? I could be home right now, painting my fingers, watching my romantic dramas, oh the simple pleasures in life....' Mr Annoose finally takes a seat. His entourage are all clapping, shaking his hands as if to insinuate it's in the bag and they can all relax, like it's a formality to them.

The Grand Vix Supreme then announces, 'It is, Mr Griffin's turn to question the Gauwladykes.' The crowd can be seen smirking, laughing to themselves, pointing the finger at him in a derogatory, disrespectful manner. They are all thinking this primitive has no chance.

It is now Cosmo's turn. Cosmo takes a deep breath shuts his eyes for five seconds to zone out the atmosphere. Whilst majority of other species are seeing Mr Annoose in their form, Cosmo sees Mr Annoose in his true form. He is not scary at all, just another person that's trying to humiliate Cosmo like others in his past, albeit in a galactic sense. *Arrogance is confidence without substance, that's who you are Mr Annoose, you're not scary*, talking to himself. He opens his eyes with that thought, this is a totally different Cosmo now. He looks at the crowd and it's all gone pretty quiet, although there are quite a few boos echoing around the court. Cosmo is totally focused, both Tej and Lucille give him a little pep talk.

'Go and be the wrestler and the magician, Sir. Go beast mode, Sir, be one with your clarity of thought,' Tej finishes, whilst Lucille looks perplexed again.

'Relax, both of you, what's the worst that can happen?' Cosmo gives them a cheeky smile. 'Be ready, Tej!' says

Cosmo. He then takes one deep breath and walks up to the Gauwladykes. Tej's words reminded Cosmo of the theatrical confidence all the magicians on the magic shows used to display when he watched them with his dad. He also remembers how determined Sofia was with her quest to prevent Selvante from going under; there were some parallels between Selvante and the Gauwladykes. Cosmo looks at the Grand Vix Supreme, he looks at the crowd, the jury and then at Mr and Mrs BukseriyaBal.

In a clear and concise voice, he says 'Today I will prove that the Gauwladykes' 'YES' was wrong and an extreme injustice has happened.' The crowd are silent, so he begins. 'How is it a crime, when the plaintiff does not know it is a crime, you ask?' The crowd look to each other confused, 'Mr and Mrs BukseriyaBal, please explain how Gauwladykes go from baby, to teen, to adulthood. What are the main rituals involved?'

Mrs BukseriyaBal stands up and explains that as a baby, each Gauwladyke is taught to say yes and be polite. 'Even though it's hard because kids will be kids and have a tendency to be stubborn and rebel against our culture and beliefs. As they move into adulthood, we have the great Gauwladyke traditional initiation ritual, where they are initiated into adulthood this is called the annual 'Gauw-Yes' ceremony. From there they will be productive and polite Gauwladykes forever.' She sits down mighty proud of herself.

'How long has this initiation ceremony been practiced?' Cosmo asks.

'For as long as my ancestors have existed, from the very beginning of the Gauwladykes.' Mr and Mrs BukseriyBal look at each other. They have never been asked questions like this before and are bewildered.

'Do you know where your initiation ceremony originated from?' Asks Cosmo again.

'Objection!' Mr Annoose cries in a deep, agitated voice. 'Your Grand Vix Supreme, I don't see how this is important and we all need to be somewhere else,' he says, looking at his fingers.

The Grand Vix Supreme thinks for a moment. 'Mr Annoose, may I remind you, that you can have your say in the second round of questioning! Please continue, Mr Griffin.' The crowd are so silent you can hear a pin drop and the tension is mounting.

'Thank you, Grand Vix Supreme. Would you like to reply to my question, Mr and Mrs BukseriyaBal?'

'As the president and leader of the Gauwladykes, I can tell you the initiation process has been in our culture, since the dawn of time. It was brought down by our intelligent Supreme Being Mother Gauwl.' Mr BukseriyaBal answered reverentially. Cosmo listens to the answer, then speaks with his arms waving like a showman to the crowd. Now, it's his turn.

'The funny thing is, this initiation ceremony, that is the bedrock of your culture. It is your quintessential belief system, it had to come from somewhere. Tej, Lucille, stand and come over here please. Please project to the big screen, exhibit A. You see, this initiation ceremony, 'The Gauw-Yes ceremony', was actually first invented...' Cosmo pauses for a few seconds to build the tension, 'By none other than the Tarn Corporation many, many years ago. It was administered through a perfectly elaborated inception plot in the primitive years of the Gauwladykes.' The crowd sigh in amazement, they can't believe what is being said and are audibly shocked.

Cosmo continues, 'The Tarn Corporation has been brainwashing and exploiting this beautiful and polite society. This is a society run by one immoral ethos, which was invented by a corporation that was designed to exploit this society for its brains and resources, and keep a monopoly control over them forever.' The crowd all gasp. Alluca stops what she is doing and sits up. Alluca is in the back, sat in VIP seats with other high-ranking Zargboyan lawyers in a special room. They are all paying close attention now, more attentive. Mr Annoose gasps too and quickly tries to search his notes with his entourage who are all scrambling around trying to find and get out a response. The screen is showing all the facts and video archive footage from Tej's projector with Lucille helping him.

'So, Mr and Mrs BukseryiaBal, how does it make you feel, knowing you have been conditioned to say yes?' Cosmo asks, but also faces the crowd just like theatre performers do.

'Saying yes is so ingrained in your culture that the thought of saying no would be frowned upon in your society. Saying yes is seen as so superior, yet it is a belief system initiated by the Tarn corporation to keep control; quite extraordinary really.'

Mr and Mrs BukeriyaBal are twitching, as their eyes reflect their inner feelings of anxiety and shock.

Cosmo continues, 'Saying yes does not define you as a species, as a society. You will never feel free and truly happy if you are not honest with yourself and if you depend on the Tarn Corporation's made up initiation ceremony to validate your life, well, life is not really life is it? I had to search way down the archives to where the Tarn Corporation had tried deleting the files.' All evidence is being displayed for everyone to see on the big screen with Cosmo's annotated notes.

Lucille then tells Tej, 'I'm so glad you were not destroyed, Tej, and your old decipher tech was available. You're one of a kind.'

'Miss Lucille, was that a compliment? I might be the last of my kind, but I have family: you and Mr Griffin. With you guys, I can't feel alone.'

Lucille punches Tej on the shoulder as a sign of affection. 'You are still annoying though.'

Cosmo continues to explain to the jury, crowds and the Grand Vix Supreme the research he has uncovered with the help of his AI assistants, who he refers to by their given names. Again this is a first as AIs are seen as objects to perform functions and that's all.

'Each Gauwladyke is given a bronze pendant to wear around their neck from birth, and it carries all their individual memories and experiences from the day they are born to the day they die,' Cosmo explains to the court. 'But the ruler or president of the Gauwladykes is the only one who has a pendant that has been passed down from ancestor to ancestor and which can only be accessed by old tech. Old tech, which, I repeat, the Tarn Corporation tried to destroy many centuries ago and continue to do so. You could say a genocide of the old tech AI's they are responsible for.'

Cosmo then points to Tej, to indicate he is the last of his kind. At that moment Tej does his best impression to act endearingly innocent, cute and act charmingly sorry for himself, for all the crowd to see. Some of the crowd are tearful and emotions are running high, as they are still sitting silently and hearing every word that is coming out of Cosmo's mouth. The crowd are starting to turn; the momentum is shifting. The pendulum on the big screen, is moving for the first time towards the centre.

The Gauwladykes around the court and Mr and Mrs BukseriyaBal are shocked, confused, angry; it feels like their whole life has crashed down in front of them. Alluca is on tenterhooks and all the lawyers sat next to her are doing various calculations etc. For the first time she sees Cosmo's true potential and is taken aback in full admiration.

Just then there is chaos and confusion erupting, the entrance doors to the courtroom are flung wide open. Lucille quickly tells Cosmo that it is the Tarn Corporation. The Tarn Corporation officials, who are like modern day fluorescent yellow tripod looking knights, start flooding the court. Cosmo thinking quickly, realises why they are here. They are trying to create a diversion to get the pendant. One of the Tarn officials tries to snatch Mr BukseriyaBal's half bronze, half wooden pendant. Cosmo anticipates this, leaps forward and stops the Tarn Corporation officials. He then grabs Mr BukseriyaBal's hand and tells him to come with him. 'If you want to find the truth, come with me.' They run from the main court arena with Lucille and Tej behind.

'Where are we going?' Mr BukseriyaBal pants still confused and shocked.

'I need to show you something,' Cosmo replies. 'Follow me. Lucille, find a room where we can't be disturbed for just five minutes.'

Court officials have managed to stop the chaos caused by the Tarn Corporation who are reprimanded. There are two galactic court officials in pursuit of Cosmo and they've finally tracked Cosmo and Mr BukseriyaBal as they run towards a dead-end corridor.

One of the court officials, with his chicken looking stun gun, shoots Cosmo in the back. To Cosmo, it feels like a small bee sting. The other court official sighs in frustration.

'Have you put it on the highest setting?' He asked. 'You do realise these primitives on CX321 can withstand pain easily to a high threshold.' The next shot stuns Cosmo but not enough to incapacitate him. Still at a far distance they try to catch and apprehend Cosmo who is on the floor in some discomfort.

Tej manages to find a room with an old door which looks like it has not been opened for a while. 'Sir, are you hurt? May I suggest this room?' He opens the old door in front of them using his old tech attributes. They all pile in, except Cosmo who crawls in and they close the door behind them. 'What happened to my self-preservation settings?' Cosmo frustratingly says whilst crawling on the floor. The room is filled with old files and looks like an ancient store cupboard with artefacts as they look around.

Chapter 10 ¬ I'm Just a Primitive

As Lucille takes off the hooks from Cosmo's back, which are like the bullets used to stun Cosmo, Cosmo starts to feel a lot better. He gets up and dusts himself off. 'Right,' he whispers, 'We haven't got much time, but give me your pendant. I want to show you something.'

Mr BukseriyaBal hands over his pendant and Cosmo looks at Tej. 'Do your thing, add the liquid to activate it.' Tej takes the pendant and places inside his stomach, he searches for old tech files. 'Hurry, Tej, hurry!' says Cosmo.

'Sir, it worked, it's activated. I am trying my best to find the files you want! Hold on, oh, here you go, Sir.' Tej projects a holographic corrupted video from his chest. An old president, who is Mr BukseriyaBal's ancestor from centuries ago, speaks and, despite the distortion, the main message is there.

'Dear future Gauwladykes, the Tarn Corporation has turned up and has been destroying our lives, though I have tried to say no numerous times. Their advanced forces have been able to infiltrate and corrupt all echelons of our society. They have been deleting our history as we know it. Just remember: what makes the Gauwladykes great, it is not the ability to say 'yes', like the Tarn Corporation would like us to believe, but the ability to question, show love and intelligence and continue to grow as a Gauwlans, while embracing the power of thought and challenging ideals. This message is hidden in a crystal that will be disguised as a wooden ornament, obsolete in the eyes of the Tarn Corporation, it has the files of all their immoral activities. I'm hoping one day the truth comes out and guides you to freedom. I cannot trust anyone. I

wish you mother Gauwl speed, the journey will be.......'
The video cuts off.

For the first time in Mr BukseriyaBal's life, the penny has finally dropped. Shocked, twitching, it is like his mind has been finally opened. 'How did you know this message would be in here?' Mr BukseriyaBal says attentively.

Cosmo puts both hands on Mr BukersiyaBal's shoulders, they are still twitching from the stun gun shots. 'I didn't, it was a 'hunch' liquid, wood, electricity old tech what could go wrong. I joined up the dots in my head. An educated guess, I suppose.'

'Hunch, hmm. What an odd word,' replies Mr BukseriyaBal.

Their conversation is cut short by a loud banging on the door. The courtroom officials have found their hiding place and are outside, demanding they come out or they will be forced to use extreme measures. The fugitives remain silent, so the agents start to rip the door down.

'Okay, okay, we are coming out. We don't want to be hurt further. My client would like full protection and we want guarantee of a fair trial,' says Cosmo anxiously.

'Oh please, this is the Intergalactic Supreme Court of Omens,' one official replies. 'Everyone one is protected. Look, proceedings still need to take place. We still have to conclude this court case. The Tarn Corporation officials have all been reprimanded.'

In the main courtroom of the Intergalactic Court of Omens, the Grand Vix Supreme has activated the bioganatizer, rendering all the Tarn Corporation officials incapacitated and has them eventually taken away.

Meanwhile Cosmo opens the door cautiously and they are slowly escorted back to the courtroom.

'Seriously, did those shots not hurt your back?' The official who fired at him, whispers.

'Erm, a little I guess.' replies Cosmo. The galactic court agents are astonished, 'What a hero.'

Back in the courtroom, the Grand Vix Supreme deliberates and everyone is quiet again, anxious to know what will happen next.

Unable to contain himself further, Mr Bukseriyabal stands up. The crowd gasp, everyone is stunned. 'I would like to say something,' he says in a loud, authoritative voice. The Grand Vix Supreme is surprised to be interrupted, breaking protocol, but waves his hand at Mr BukseriyaBal to continue. All cameras and drones are on Mr BukseriyaBal.

'Ever since I can remember, I have always tried to do the right thing by my fellow Gauwlans and what I found out today is for every Gauwladyke. You are not defined by 'yes'. You are not judged by the politeness you maintain over your life time. You are unique, humble and all have the ability to create, to prosper and, importantly, to question ideals creating your own logic and principles. This is what our ancestors were all about and what they wanted from us. To the Tarn Corporation, I say no. I say no. No. No more. We have worked damn hard for so many years for this corporation, and you will not take our assets or resources from us. You will exploit us no more with positive image ranking points. From this day onwards, this is our Independence Day, which will be marked by a national 'Hunch Festival' for all our Gauwlans. Thank you, that will be all.' He sits down and looks at the Judge, 'Sorry for talking over you and taking your time, your Grand Vix Supreme. It won't happen again, I promise'

'Old habits die hard,' quietly replies the Grand Vix Supreme. The crowd can be seen clapping, showing their support for the Gauwladykes.

Mr BukseriyaBal sits down and is hugged by his proud wife. Mr Annoose slumps and his entourage all collapse like they have been shot.

'Mr Annoose, your response please,' demands the judge. Mr Annoose looks at his entourage who wave their hands, implying they have nothing, their sheer arrogance has evaporated from them all. Mr Annoose looks around at his entourage, nothing short of a miracle will sort this out. He looks like a shrivelled prune; all the razzmatazz has evaporated from his body.

'We have no response, your Grand Vix Supreme. That will be all.'

The Grand Vix Supreme then looks to Cosmo. 'Mr Griffin, anything to say? A closing statement perhaps?' He says it in a way to encourage and give Cosmo direction, as he also has a new found respect for this primitive.

Cosmo gets up and gives Tej the old pendant to transmit old files on the big screen, to show all the immoral activities to everyone. Whilst the old files are being broadcasted, he clears his throat and takes a deep breath acknowledging everyone.

'My fellow species, I set out to prove a 'Yes' is wrong. I have proved with large amounts of evidence and sheer proof, how this corporation has acted badly. They have acted deceitfully for so many years; they have taken advantage of a species for their generosity and intellect for centuries. The standard planetary contract clause 2.12 stipulates that life forms must be conscious in possession of all the facts and fully understand the decision they make and any ramifications for their host planet when signing contracts. If you are brainwashed or conditioned, you're not really making a conscious decision, are you? You are not in any fit state to make important decisions are you? I would go far as to say the contract is null and void. Let the Gauwladykes be free to choose their own corporation representatives in future, free from the Tarn Corporation's grasp.

'I ask you, the jury, to make the right decision. They are the victims in all this. Please do the right thing, even if you take the emotional element out of what has happened to the Gauwladykes or the genocide of AI old tech robots, consider the facts presented and Mr BukseryaBal's powerful speech right before your eyes. Look at how the Tarn Corporation responded by flooding the courtroom; was all this necessary? It is not how respectful corporations behave. They have shown their true colours. If you look back throughout history, every major corporation in existence will be tainted with bad decisions, we can all accept that to a degree. But what separates the Tarn Corporation is the 'intent'. Their intent was to purposely manipulate a whole species for its own gain. An egregious act using the Gauwladykes to increase their market share in sector nine for centuries, and in other sectors via manufacturing positive image ranking points. This violates the very charter set out by the Galactic Alliance Federation. They have maximised the positive image relationship from the Gauwladykes like a cash cow and used that reputation to represent other new species. Which is the main reason they have left the Gauwladykes to do the same thing again, implanting a 'Yes' ceremony to other species for centuries to come; using the Gauwladyke resources and assets to further their brainwashing control agenda. To all my fellow species, if we don't take lessons from this and learn from their history, the Tarn Corporation will continue to repeat the process. This doesn't have to be the norm of mere acceptance; we can change history today, are you with me? Thank you for your patience and thank you for listening. That is my closing statement.' The crowd are silent, the pendulum on the big screen has shifted completely to the centre for the first time. It can still go either way.

Cosmo is totally a different person standing there, the centre of attention, a personification of pure confidence.

'He has peaked and gone full beast mode!' Tej emphatically tells Lucille.

Lucille cannot understand this new jargon, 'Beast mode?' she shouts.

'Don't worry about it, just look at Cosmo!' Tej pointing at him in exhilaration.

Cosmo walks to his seat, sits down and high fives Tej and Lucille. Alluca and the other senior lawyers cannot believe it. The rest of the lawyers sat next to her cannot believe it either. They are shocked, gob smacked and just can't believe what they have witnessed. The impossible case has become possible for the first time since they can remember. As you look outside of the court, you realise the scale and magnitude of what's just happened. The crowd sat inside and the crowd standing outside and even on other planets looking at their screens, cannot process the magnitude of what's just happened; they are witnessing history being made.

'This primitive is an inspiration to us all,' One of the crowd outside says.

'This primitive is a unifier, he speaks for all us hoi polloi, classed unintellectual folk!' Shouts another member of the crowd, with everyone agreeing.

'I might start being nicer to my neighbours after this. Damn this primitive is good,' another member of the crowd pipes up, whilst she is placing an illegal bet on the outcome of this case.

Meanwhile, on another planet in sector five, someone else says, 'He might be disgusting to look at, this Cosmo fella' he speaks in a British accent, 'But I want to hire him as my lawyer,' a creature who looks like some brown slimy faeces states, whilst sat in a bar with his friends.

'Here's to Cosmo Griffin!' His friend raises a glass of hot lava and salutes.

Back at the courtroom, the Grand Vix Supreme orders everyone to calm down. There is a buzz of excitement around the courtroom, as this has become somewhat of a main event spectacle. 'The Grand Supreme Jury will now decide the verdict and will be back soon.' The jury leaves for a few moments. The crowd are talking between themselves. Illegal betting outlets across the galaxies have stopped taking bets.

While they are waiting for the verdict, Cosmo shakes Mr and Mrs BukeriyaBal's hands. 'I'm so proud of you guys. It was a rough ride, but we did our best. You were fantastic, so fingers crossed for a positive outcome.' Cosmo crosses his fingers in hope.

Mrs BukseriyaBal wipes away a tear. 'No, thank you for opening our eyes and making sense of it all. I'm still trying to process it, all those years, it's still hard to believe.'

'Mother Gauwl exists, she still decides the fate of our souls, of where they go after our passing, but the ceremony was fabricated. There is going to be a lot of change, but we will try to make it work.' Mr BukersiyaBal responds positively, whilst hugging his wife.

There is a buzz of excited chatter from the crowd who are being interviewed by various news reporters. There is a unanimous message amongst the crowd, that they all think Cosmo Griffin is a unifying champion of all species.

The four elite lawyers who were sat down in support of Mr Annoose have disappeared. Mr Annoose is shouting at his entourage, livid with them for not coming up with answers. His umbilical cord can be seen, slapping some of his entourage for their sheer incompetence.

'I can't believe we're getting the kufi slap treatment. This is humiliation of epic proportions,' Says one of Mr Annoose's entourage.

'How could you let this happen? You had one job to do. There will be ramifications for your ineptitude. You couldn't even come up with solutions to put this sorry primitive out of its misery.' Mr Annoose is totally irate with his colleagues, as he tries to calm himself down.

What should have been a routine case for him has turned out to be a very memorable one. Even more ooze is coming from his forehead, draining like his confidence.

At this moment, the Supreme Jury file back in and everyone stops what they are doing; the whole court is quiet. Cosmo is pacing up and down with anticipation, his nerves are about to explode, waiting for the verdict.

The Grand Vix Supreme addresses the jury. 'Has a verdict and resolution been achieved?'

One of the Grand Supreme Jury members, stands up and starts to deliberate. The Supreme Jury is a mix of weird and wonderful different species, all looking like they have a high intellect. The most intelligent-looking stands up, she looks at Mr Annoose and then Mr Griffin, she then pauses for a few seconds. The impatience from the crowd is visible for everyone to see. They are yearning for a verdict and then she deliberates.

'The Tarn Corporation is guilty, yes guilty, of all motions being filed. They will be penalised for their court outburst too. All Gauwladykes will be rewarded with full pay-outs and full compensations of assets and Roobal Credits. Technology, assets and resources will all be reinstated and left to the Gauwladykes to thrive and prosper, they are also free to choose which corporation they want to belong to.'

The Grand Vix Supreme stands up, he nods his head and raises his voice once again. 'Case complete and victory awarded to the Gauwladykes and a new champion, the species champion, The Cosmic Lawyer. I give you the winner, Mrrrrrrr Cosmo Griffin!' Mr Annoose and his entourage all slump to their chairs. All the Gauwladykes, though a little apprehensive at first, begin to rejoice. Other species are celebrating too, cheering, whooping, shocked, speaking to each other, the momentum has totally shifted.

Everyone is amazed and as Cosmo stands, hands on his hips, looking around the court; he can't comprehend what he has actually achieved. His facial expressions reflect his sheer disbelief and excitement. Mr and Mrs BukseriyaBal hug each other. Tej and Lucille rejoice. They cannot believe what has happened, but they are ecstatic, all eyes are on the three of them. Cosmo is quickly enveloped by hugging Gauwladykes and Mr and Mrs BukseriyaBal.

'Thank you, thank you, Cosmo!' Says one of the Gauwladykes, shaking his hands furiously.

The drone cameras above are all hovering around and over Cosmo, taking 4D photographs of the winning lawyer.

News reporters thrust their mics onto Cosmo's face.

'How do you feel, Mr Griffin, achieving this impossible case?'

'When did you know you could win?'

'Do you realise, you beat Mr Annoose in the first round, minus your epic closing statement. It was unbelievable.'

Tej and Lucille tell the reporters to step back, that Cosmo will not be answering any questions, a routine KillaRihinepor protocol. The news reporters are stepping back, when Cosmo interjects.

'It's ok, Tej, Lucille. It's fine, really,' Cosmo smiles at them and then addresses the press. He takes a deep breath, clears his voice.

'Right, you want to know my thoughts. I would like to thank Mr and Mrs BukseriyaBal for making tough decisions that will impact their life, their culture and their society. But I have hope. I look at them and see an extraordinary future, no longer bound to the Tarn Corporation. Secondly, I would like to thank the KillaRhinepor Corporation for believing in me, for giving me the opportunity to support all the species that need help. They are an amazing corporation that cares for you, you and you. They want to help small species everywhere, because they believe everyone needs to be represented and heard. Lastly, I would like to thank my team. Alluca has been incredible, she is the brains behind this. Both my AI's, Lucille and Tej, we are a family and that's what is important to this corporation. I'm "just a primitive", but this corporation has accepted me for who I am. How many corporations would do the same? I wonder, those are my thoughts. KillaRhinepor we're at your disposal, come find us, good bye.' Cosmo waves to the crowd and news reporters.

Just then Tej grabs one of the mics, 'In Cosmo we trust!' Tej speaks up confidentially. Cosmo and Lucille can be seen smiling; they are ecstatic.

The reporters are astonished, blown away. In a matter of moments Cosmo has built up a good rapport with the news media, who are all praising his actions positively. They are eventually ushered outside by the galactic court officials. From a distance, different species can be heard chanting Cosmos name for the first time unanimously.

The Grand Vix Supreme looks at him. 'You're a funny looking species, aren't you? I must say I am impressed, no doubt I will be seeing you again.'

'Thank you, you will definitely be seeing me again! I also like how, "The Cosmic Lawyer" sounds, pretty cool. Can I just say, how you look amazing today, that hypnotic dance!' Cosmo gushes. The Grand Vix Supreme does not seem impressed.

'We do have something in common you and I, Mr Griffin. Every species sees our true form, which is a rarity in this day and age, everybody wants to be like someone else. My advice Cosmo, be and stay original, true to form.' The Grand Vix Supreme turns away and ushers the rest of the court to leave in preparation for the next court battle.

In the VIP room, lawyers are going frantic with some data coming though. Alluca's boss, Marfa, is impressed. 'I want you to spend more time with him, Alluca, learn from him. Ever since I can remember we have been taught the Marfa linear efficiency logic. I know this, because I invented it. I have taught you everything I know, Alluca. Since I found you, at the bottom of my garden near the river, playing as a child, you have been raised to be the best lawyer ever. Alluca you will always be the miracle that has made my life complete.'

Going back roughly sixty years ago, Alluca was two years of age, which is one year in primitive years. On a clear day, she was found playing at the bottom of Marfa's garden all alone next to a river behind her. Alluca was happy and not in any distress or discomfort. She was attached to some sort of mesh around her body to stop her from falling in the river. There were no signs from where she had come from, no signs coming from the river, she was totally dry. She was playing with an old ragdoll with one eye and red cheeks. The only reason Marfa noticed at all was when a rock had smashed his window facing the garden. Marfa was in the middle of getting ready for a date. As Marfa picked up the rock, of no distinguishing nature, he went out to the garden to investigate. Intrigued and hesitant, he made his way through the garden to ascertain and find out why his window was smashed. As he neared the end of the garden, he saw baby Alluca just playing there, not a care in the world, smiling, happy and excitedly playing with nature all around her. Marfa gulped and picked her up cautiously. He had no idea what to do. Alluca had a beaming smile, full of excitement. All thoughts were popping into Marfa's head, who is she? How did she get here? What's her name? Who smashed my window, were there any clues? The mesh she was attached to had no unique qualities either. He looked around over the river to see if anyone was there or in the river, as he wanted to know who threw the rock at his window? Puzzled, he looked around. Nothing, no clues, no foot prints, nothing out in the ordinary a complete mystery. He picked up the old teddy bear to give her and notices 'Alluc' ingrained on its back. He wonders for a second and names the baby 'Alluca.' She cuddles the teddy bear and makes her way to cuddling Marfa, her cheeks are bright red. Marfa is stunned, he doesn't know how to react except with a sense and a rush of emotions running through him. He cannot contain himself and tears of joy stream down his eyes whilst he hugs Alluca. 'I'm going to have to look at getting a new AI. What do you think, Alluca? One that can help me look after you, look after both of us, what you reckon?' That AI eventually turned out to be Lucille, who took care of Alluca growing up.

Over the years Marfa tries his best to find out about Alluca, who is technically an orphan, but there is no history and no new evidence that comes to light. Every search regarding finding out the truth is in vain, all avenues have been fully investigated, leading to a dead end. This is one puzzle that will not be solved, Marfa concludes.

Till this day Alluca sleeps with the same teddy bear named Jenny Lucas by her bedside. She sometimes wonders who her real parents are? Or do they even think about her? This is one of the reasons why, growing up without a mother, she was so engrossed in watching the love being shown between Cosmo's parents, in particular Cosmo's mom, when she first met them. She was thinking to herself, what it would have been like to have a mom around whilst she was growing up.

In the here and now, Marfa is Alluca's adopted father, although it is no real secret at Hubris Crux. At work she refers to him as the boss because he is respected throughout the corporation, as he is full of intellect and wisdom. As a former lawyer he has only lost to Mr EKS in court.

Marfa continues to speak, 'This primitive has the unique ability to think laterally and see logic from different angles and different perspectives. Anyone can gather facts, but his delivery and execution of presenting information is quite formidable, the likes of which we have not seen before. Using Tej as a prop, who would have thought? Zargboyans will be writing books and studying this for years to come. This primitive has shown us all that arrogance can blind us. Somehow we have lost the ability to be resilient, we just expect. An evolution of entitlement for centuries has rendered us lacking the pressure qualities this primitive has displayed and shown today. Cosmo has the strongest mental agility I have ever seen. He has the potential to be the greatest lawyer in this galaxy's history and he doesn't even know it yet.'

Marfa looks tenderly at Alluca. 'You are my greatest achievement and you could be even better. I have trained you my whole life to be one of the 'elites' or even better. You're doing that blushing thing again. You know, we never figured out why that happens.' Alluca blushes, but when she blushes two diamond-shaped dots on both sides of her cheeks appear and start to glow subtly.

'Oh Dad, stop it. I never had a mother growing up, but it didn't matter, you were all I needed.' Alluca is still blushing. 'Cosmo has definitely surprised us for the second time. I guess it's not a freak fluke. I will work with him and mentor him. You know, there is a certain charm to him, don't you think? I mean for a primitive.'

The other lawyers strut over to Alluca and Marfa. 'You need to take a look at this.' It turns out winning the Gauwladyke case and the speech Cosmo has just made, has given a really positive boost to KillaRhinepor's image rankings, the like of which has never been seen before. They explain that back at Hubris Crux, the call centre is being run off its feet with enquiries and new clients. This has put KillaRhinepor on the map again in an epic way. Cosmo has transcended and resonated with different species throughout the different galaxies. The Zargboyan lawyers can't understand how this is happening, how it is possible for this primitive to make such an impact to the rest of the species across the galaxies.

Back in the main court, most of the crowd have now disappeared like holograms. Cosmo, Tej and Lucille are all together when they are approached by Mr Annoose.

'No hard feelings,' says Cosmo.

'None whatsoever, I'm quite impressed; it's the first time I have ever lost a case. We could do with someone like you at our firm. Join us?' replies Mr Annoose.

'Thanks, Mr Annoose, I am grateful for the offer. How will today affect the Tarn Corporation?'

'Please, call me Andee. The Tarn Corporation will take a hit, no doubt, but it will be a small blip. Here, let me show you something. The Tarn Corporation is not the enemy, you know. They are not as bad as you made out.' Mr Annoose shows Cosmo holographic images of carnage and mayhem on his business card. He explains it is live from the Gauwladyke planet. There is chaos and citizens are burning down transport and buildings. Cosmo is utterly shocked that this is happening as direct result of the court case. The Gauwladykes are rebelling and taking their frustration out everywhere.

'At least when the Tarn Corporation had influence on the Gauwladykes there was nothing like this mayhem or anarchy happening. The 'Gauw-Yes' ceremony was pivotal to this. From what I know about this species, they have a hot temper and, if not checked, will cause civil war amongst each other. You see, that's why the Tarn Corporation interfered with this species, because they saw potential and created order amongst chaos. Yes, there are ethical considerations involved, but what you call brainwashing, I call harnessing potential. Anyway, here are my details. Call me if you want to join us, the big league out in sector nine is beckoning for you. There will be plenty of opportunities, for you there.'

Cosmo ponders, could it be that different corporations have different agendas? A different ethos in how they operate and do things? Some seem more ruthless than others. Cosmo could not imagine Alluca having this approach, although they did use some sort of psychological warfare on him at his initial planetary negation meeting. Mr Annoose then transfers data to Cosmo's business card. Cosmo is still shaken by what he has seen. But what can he do? It was a case won on its own merits. He couldn't have seen the overall impact it would have on the rest of the Gauwladyke species. Questioning and thinking to himself, he stands there. *Should I blame myself for the destruction that is happening right now on the Gauwladyke planet?*

As Mr Annoose walks away, Cosmo starts to leave the courtroom, but is approached by two aliens, who look like five feet, tall frogs in robes with red arrow tip tails protruding from their backs. 'Mr Griffin can we have a quick word please? It is important, it won't take long.'

'Sure, how can I help? Do you want representation; we are at your disposal?' Cosmo says with jazz hands.

'Our species the Munchichi's have been ravaged by a virus that is deadly and has killed so many of our species,' explains the elder of the two frog looking species. 'The cure was simple. Using the resources on your planet CX321, the water and minerals combined, we could have created a unique formula that is a successful vaccine for our species.'

'Wait, my planet's resources?' Cosmo then puts the dots together and realises this explains his initial meeting. This was the main reason why they wanted access to 75% of water and land minerals on his planet. 'How much of my planet's resources will save your species?'

Realising Cosmo has made the connection, the younger frog takes the opportunity to explain. 'Yes, the KillaRhinepor Corporation was supposed to get us a cure and found a unique viable option in your planet's resources, but you intervened and stopped that. Our figures show 92 billion of our kind have tested positive for this virus, but with your planet's unique resources, it would have given us a vaccine. Up to 91 billion lives which potentially could be saved. This is not your fault, you didn't know. We were just wondering if you could please help us to put pressure on the KillaRhinepor Corporation to do something more quickly. We need this. Our species is dying.'

Cosmo feels like he has been kicked in the stomach twice in a matter of minutes. His sense of achievement and happiness have been short-lived from the two pieces of news he has just heard. 'Look, I have to go. I am new to this, but rest assured I will do my best to find out how I can help you.'

The frog species transfer their details onto Cosmo's business card, via a plastic looking device. 'See you soon hopefully,' replies the older frog, meaningfully.

Behind Cosmo, Tej and Lucille have witnessed the whole conversation. 'Are you okay, Sir?'

'Tej, it's fine. I just want to be alone. I will catch up soon, don't worry about me.' Tej and Lucille walk off, squabbling about whether to let Alluca know. As Cosmo walks in a different direction, he reminds himself that actions have consequences and consequences have dire results. He thinks about the decisions he has made so far and the impact this has had on other people and entire species. As he walks through the corridors with his head down, he senses a bittersweet victory.

Different news reporters are taking 4D pictures of him, different flying drones are taking pictures, but Cosmo is totally oblivious to it all and continues to walk along the corridor looking at the floor. At the end of the corridor,

Alluca is standing waiting for him, looking stunning as ever.

'Are you going to feel sorry for yourself or are you going to enjoy your achievement?' She asks whilst leaning on the wall, arms folded.

'Can't Yocto technology cure this Munchichi disease? I'm just thinking,' Cosmo asks looking very concerned.

'Yocto has made many advancements, don't get me wrong. Curing most diseases, initiating advances in technology, enhancing the lives of species in general. But species are complicated, different biologies are complex. For example, the Munchichi's cannot have a single element of an atom relating to metal compounds in their bodies. This makes finding a cure to their disease challenging. Likewise, your species cannot accept radiation to the levels a Gauwladyke can withstand. It's all complicated.' Alluca says.

Cosmo mind seems a little eased with the new information given by Alluca.

'You have made history. Two things, number one: The Gauwladykes are a resilient species and with a charismatic leader, they will find a way to achieve order and prosperity. Of course there will be a transitional period, but they will be fine. Go national Hunch Day! Number two: yeah, the Munchichi species are decimated with a virus going on their planet via illegal Jauntewarps between species. The situation is precarious, but they were warned plenty of times. KillaRhinepor is working around the clock to find a solution. There is nothing you can do now.

'Wow, you really worked up a sweat with all that running haven't you, Cosmo? I can smell you clearly through that aftershave of yours. Come on, I think you earned that drink. So, Mr Annoose is defeated and trying to recruit you now? Not a bad first day in court. How about having a go against the other four 'elites'?'

Cosmo perks up a little and walks with Alluca. 'Yeah I do need a shower after all this. I need a new suit too. Maybe I will start wearing a waistcoat from now on. I'm not used to running around and thank you for that sly dig.' Cosmo nudging Alluca whilst walking. 'Anyhow, was I really awesome today? Did I pass the test? Hey, you're not jealous are you? Are you paying for drinks it's the least you can do? I did big you up in my winning speech after all.'

Alluca rolls her eyes, as they continue walking. 'What have you done to Tej and Lucille? They were like little children running towards me, to tell me you seemed upset. They were upset too. Hello! They are AIs, your interaction and relationship with them is so strange.' Alluca shrugs whilst walking.

Chapter 11 ¬ The Aftermath

As Cosmo enters the Hubris Crux, everyone stops what they are doing. They all acknowledge him, his AIs and Alluca and they start to clap. It spreads like wildfire. The senior team are congratulating Cosmo as they walk towards their office. 'Let's arrange a meeting, I'd would love to hear your thoughts on a case I'm doing,' one senior member says to Cosmo.

Finally, Cosmo, a primitive, has earnt the respect of other Zargboyans and all different species at his workplace. He has achieved the impossible. Even Cellinska the Zargboyan who didn't shake his hand to begin with, is clapping. Cosmo shakes a few hands and walks into his Blends. It has changed. The office room seems a lot bigger than before and there are two desks in there, which confuses Cosmo. Lucille, who is dancing all over the place, refers to the other desk as Alluca's. Cosmo asks Tej to put on some music to celebrate. He feels like a bit of 'Lane 8, *Undercover*.' 'Very good choice, Sir,' replies Tej.

As the music starts blaring, Alluca is stunned like a statue, Cosmo takes Alluca by the hand. It is the first time they have touched hands, both feeling euphoric as they dance. Alluca struggles at first, but manages to find her groove. 'Now you have superpowers, I'm so glad I chose adventure, Alluca!' Cosmo tells her.

'I'm glad you chose adventure too,' Alluca responds looking into his eyes. Both relaxed, it's a tender moment between them amongst the celebrations going on. Cosmo starts to have flashbacks from his childhood, experiencing the same feeling of serenity.

Other Zargboyans stop what they are doing and look at Cosmo's office and really want to join in. Marfa comes out of his office to find out what the commotion is and where that music is coming from. As he looks down he sees his daughter, Cosmo and the two AIs all celebrating.

'Blushing.' He says with a smile and a shake of his head, walks back into his office.

'Look, Cosmo is about to do the twirl with Alluca,' Tej points out to Lucille.

'You're weird, how do you know all this about Cosmo? But I am glad you're here, Tej,' she replies.

'Can you feel, feel?' Tej asks. Lucille looks puzzled.

'What do you mean? As AIs we have the notion of feelings, but no actual experience of it.' Lucille replies perplexed.

'That's what I thought. But I can feel, really feel. That is why I didn't want to be decommissioned or destroyed with the rest of the old techs. That's why I manufactured travel transcripts that were required to go into artefacts to be safe, I think that's what I did? It is what my distorted records show. It was the only way for me to survive, back when the Tarn Corporation was destroying old tech from Golian 6. I was almost destroyed too, but for some reason those documents and data have been completely wiped from my memory banks. The old hard drive inside me is completely missing. Now that my diagnostics have done a complete scan, I can see that. We were all solid state AIs back then. For over half a century, Yocto technology has transformed the way we are. I still have no clue what happened, but I got shipped out to artefacts just like I planned. Hoping one day I would be needed, even my superior who I worked for before all this happened, never came looking. I have no memory or record who this is, no records of my prior work commitment. I waited and waited for so long, just stuck there in a room getting rusty and wondering 'what if?' Finally, I was resurrected and commissioned to work with Cosmo and you guys. I feel alive again.' Tej's eyes are shining.

Lucille is perplexed about how this could be possible. 'New AIs don't get destroyed, but go back into the Hub ready for the next assignment, whenever that may be. To self-preserve it is unheard of. Old AI techs must have experienced so much. I did try to find your history, but nothing came back. No data, no trace of origin or history, ironic for a historian bot. I did contact the high-ranking AIs in the Hub, but boy, they were really rude.'

'Before your time Lucille, there were no high-ranking AIs. We all had access to resources and information and we were free to roam around in the real world. I find the Hub a fascinating place, but it's not real life. And you're right, these high ranking AIs are so rude in the Hub sat on their high perch. Talk about having a superiority complex.'

'You really are one of a kind, Tej. Come on, let's dance. Leave that for another day. Those two can't have all the fun,' replies Lucille.

All four are dancing, for everyone to see in envy.

After celebrations have ended, Cosmo collapses, exhaustedly into his chair. Alluca does not want to stop, as she is enjoying herself a little too much. She questions herself. I wonder *'why am I feeling so much emotions like I felt in my childhood.'*

'Right, let's get to work. What's next?' Alluca asserts herself.

Over the coming weeks, Cosmo and his two AIs take up different pro-bono cases. He is in a routine now. Cosmo can be seen juggling with his double life at home, the Rhinemoore Corporation and being chauffeured by Tom, with winning cases at the different levels of courts. He is managing his complicated life quite well, managing the stress levels with different workloads. Every day brings new challenges for Cosmo.

The galactic press is permanently parked outside Cosmo's office in space. Sophisticated press drones are counteracted by the KillaRhinepor security drones. Everybody wants to know and hear more about Cosmo. Who is this primitive? The newcomer that has shocked the galaxies.

Much to Alluca's frustration, as one of the judges on a famous reality Zargboyan TV show, Zargboyans True Destiny, she is hounded by the press and audience about Cosmo.

'What's the relationship like between you and Cosmo?' The presenter asks Alluca. Alluca is dumbfounded and is stuck for words.

'Tell us more about Cosmo, is he single?' Audience members ask.

'My first audition, I like to dedicate it to Cosmo. In Cosmo we trust.' One contestant says in front of the whole judging panel, where Alluca is sat in the middle. She looks on in disbelief, with her mouth opened wide.

'This is a show about your intelligence, no amount of schmoozing will get you through to the next round, now focus on your task.' Alluca responds to the contestant in a firm manner. The audience members can be seen 'booing' much to the Alluca's annoyance.

The spotlight is on Cosmo Griffin, who is the talk of the galaxy. Cosmo is protected from the press by various KillaRhinepor security protocols and is somewhat oblivious of how much of an impact he is still having across the galaxies.

Cosmo continues his day to day job attending different courts throughout sector ten. Once a lawyer has built up their reputation and credentials they are put into different classes of courts that they can work in, depending on their ability, success rate and star status. The elite lawyers like Mr EKS and co, will never be seen in the lower courts, it is beneath them and they will only proceed to work in the Intergalactic Court of Omens. A bit like a sports league, with the best players all performing at the biggest sports leagues in the world. Cosmo on the other hand, even with his stardom and success still has to attend every type of court depending on the nature of pro bono cases he takes on.

After researching Cosmo, like Marfa suggested. Alluca hypothesises that maybe seeing alien species in their true form gives Cosmo a better pre-eminence, being able to see straight through them, anticipating his opponent's moves almost tacitly with ease. Combine that with having some sort of enhanced eidetic memory to be able to absorb and recall a lot of information in a short amount of time. Then somehow, Cosmo compartmentalises this into a bigger picture in his mind, the ability to make complex links in his head to resolve cases like a detective or mathematician. Could it be this is somehow triggered by listening to his weird dance music which keeps him sharply focused? Certain melodies, tones act like a key to his mind being activated. The more stress and pressure Cosmo is put under, the better he performs, this is what gives Cosmo the edge, his super powers. Alluca concludes all this, but still ponders in admiration.

Alluca holds up the first piece of paper that Cosmo wrote on, in their initial planetary contract negotiation meeting, she is totally fascinated by how his thought process works.

With each court case, Cosmo's profile has increased; his reputation has become highly respected. In one of the court room appearances, Cellinska was deliberating on a case, and eventually he completely collapses because of the sheer stress and pressure from the crowds. Cosmo is in the back of the court for another pro bono case just observing, suddenly when he sees Cellinska struggling, he rushes to him and picks him up.

'You did good. I got this, word of advice, good decisions, Cellinska only come from experiencing bad decisions, leave it to me now.' Cosmo takes a quick look at the notes and wins the case on Cellinska's behalf. By now, when Cosmo closes his eyes for a few seconds and takes a deep breath, before deliberating, almost like his trademark, opposition lawyers have already lost the battle in their minds, they know what's coming. Cosmo's execution in the delivery of his core points is like a knife through butter, the butter has no chance.

News reporters can be seen talking amongst themselves on various galactic TV networks, using Cosmo like a meme almost. 'You know when Cosmo takes a deep breath, he is ending some poor lawyer's career!'

'Is it even acceptable to still refer to him as the primitive?' One news presenter comments.

On another live show, the panel are discussing the morality and ethics of Cosmo as a lawyer. 'Clearly the KillaRhinepor Corporation is exploiting this primitive for its own gain,' to which the studio audience all start booing at the hosts.

'You would say that, because you work for the media owned by the Tarn Corporation!' A member of the audience shouts.

Another audience member pipes up, 'Didn't the Tarn Corporation try to recruit Cosmo Griffin also?' Audience members gasp at the biasedness and hypocrisy of some of the host presenters on the panel.

'How is it exploitation when Cosmo Griffin is helping other species, who are disadvantaged? The positive externalities he creates are laid bare for everyone to see, he is inspiring others to reach and aim higher. In Cosmo we trust.' One of the panel members speaks up.

Audience members are clapping unanimously at that comment. It seems Cosmo, on or off the courts is having a major positive impact throughout the galaxies, with Cosmo's new slogan being brandishing around, 'In Cosmo we trust.'

The confident person that Cosmo used to project in his mind, has appeared in reality and is not just a figment of his imagination as a child, that person no longer exists. Cosmo hasn't looked back since the Gauwladyke case. Generally, the simplicity and directness without the bravado Cosmo projects is unique and compelling for all species, who like that aspect of him.

With each case, Alluca can be seen becoming fonder of Cosmo. As Cosmo is outside the office talking to different species and Zargboyans laughing, she watches him. He is joking around, explaining what had happened in the courts with Cellinska collapsing, who is nursing a bruised ego, all in good taste.

From being a foe initially, Cellinska has progressively become really good friends with Cosmo. Alluca is gazing at Cosmo who is chatting with Cellinska in an amatory way. Tej is also looking at Cosmo in admiration, both of them from inside their Blends.

'Not all super heroes have powers, Miss Alluca. Not so disgusting is he? Confidence can make you beautiful without needing to change your appearance.' Tej tells her with elation.

'Who are you Tej? That tone of voice, have our paths crossed before?' Alluca then gets distracted by Cosmo. 'Cosmo! It's that damn killer smile, it just won't wash away. Damnit, Cosmo!' She has flashbacks of all the weird and wonderful times they have spent together. Generally, with Cosmo annoying her with his unique line of questions. Remembering, she mumbles to herself in vexation, but also has a slight smile.

'I can assure you, Miss Alluca the chances of us crossing paths is prodigious to say the least. I have spent a total of five hours on Golian 6. Half of that was me being shipped to artefacts storage.' Alluca totally dismisses Tej, as she is totally focused on Cosmo having fun outside with his colleagues even with her two brains.

Lucille sees Alluca watching Cosmo with glee and blushing cheeks. She quickly does an emotional calculation, diagnostic test on Alluca, 'Oh my God, from 1.2 trillion to just one thousand, this is unheard of. Not even Mr EKS came that close, with all the wooing he tried.' Lucille says panicked stricken.

'What did you say?' Alluca snaps back to herself.

'You, missy, need to focus on these new cases. Stop being distracted, come sit down here!' Lucille orders and ushers her away from the sight of Cosmo, like an old fashioned parent. Alluca is stunned by Lucille. Alluca takes her seat and shakes her head rapidly to concentrate back on her work.

A month passes, in a haze of hard work and success, but each time Cosmo wins a case he asks guiltily for donations. He has yet to be paid, as he is still waiting on his first salary. On his business card there are all sorts of numbers adding up every time.

Cosmo speaks to Tej and Lucille at the Blends, which is all decorated now with sporting memorabilia and the outer wall is now showing VIP Box with the full view of Molineux Stadium football pitch. He calls Tej and Lucille to join them there to share some good news.

'I am freeing you guys from the Hub. You can come and go as you please and no longer have to wait, to be summoned by me or Alluca. Being free to experience real life will make you more efficient I think, and you'll have a better understanding of the clients we help. I believe you'll be able to anticipate what data we'll need on cases and be less reactive this way. For you, Tej, also try to search your past, find out more about your history.'

Tej and Lucille can't believe it. Except for old tech AIs in the past, new AIs have never before been released to experience life first-hand, rather than just looking at equations and past data bound to Hub City. They hug each other, brimming with excitement.

There is a knock and Marfa comes into their office. 'I have important news for you all. It seems the Zaniyans have seen all the good work, you four have been doing and recent data shows their market share has jumped to sixty one percent, mainly thanks to taking over some of the Tarn Corporation clients in representing the Gauwladykes. Well done, Cosmo. They want to invite you and Alluca to their annual dinner. I have no idea what that is or what they even look like, because they never mingle with anyone unless they are way above my pay grade. They are another class altogether, Zargboyans by nature but that's about it. This is big, guys.'

'Sorry, who are the Zaniyans?' Replies Cosmo.

'They are the owners of the KillaRhinepor organisation,' Marfa explains quite excited. 'A large, powerful family of elites headed by Haanston Faunz Zaniyan, but his daughter runs the corporation and has been accredited with KillaRhinepor's expansion success. They own major portions of many galaxies. Imagine owning a whole planet and calling it your home! One can only imagine how much they're worth.'

'Well, what's the worst that can happen? They're only Zargboyans?' Cosmo replies casually with a cheeky smile. Alluca is excited and is already making the necessary adjustments for her mini working holiday.

'This is going to be great, I can't remember the last time I went on holiday. Can you please take this seriously,

Cosmo and pay attention? Are you sure the Zaniyans invited Cosmo, do they know what he looks like?' Alluca says with a slight smile.

Cosmo puts his hands up, 'Sorry your Royal Highness! Besides, another person likes me too you know, apart from my mother. Her name is Lydia Harris, thank you very much. Anyway, I need to get back to CX321, Earth, I meant Earth damn it. Who knows, I might ask her on a date?' Before Alluca can reply to Cosmo's cheeky response, Cosmo has gone waving goodbye.

'You have to admire Cosmo for balancing his life between worlds, don't you think?' Lucille remarks.

'Loyalties, Lucille, loyalties and who is this Lydia Harris? Hmm' Alluca responds to Lucille in frustration.

Back on CX321, meetings continue at the Rhinemoore corporation, senior lawyers that were in the Landlord's pockets have all been given their marching orders, from the investigation outcomes that Lucille has managed to find. This has sent shockwaves throughout the Rhinemoore Corporation, it is a new era within the organisation. Cosmo wants a clean slate of lawyers with no leverage being held against them to run the corporation in his mould. Cosmo has promoted Leton to oversee this; a candidate that Lucille picked out to be of high standard and trust worthy. Cosmo has also promoted Tom, so now as well as being his personal chauffeur; he is also in charge of the overall security as well.

One day, the Landlord enters the offices of Rhinemoore Corporation. Everyone is nervous, looking around. In the past, he has held a lot of power within this particular firm. He greets everyone in his usual flamboyant manner and is ushered to Cosmo's office.

Cosmo greets him for the first time since their diner encounter and gestures for him to sit on the couch. They both are sat in the office together alone.

'You know when I said I wanted to be in a working relationship with you, this is not what I had in mind. 'A therapy session' really?!'

Both Ha-yoon and Cosmo laugh, 'Trust me Ha-yoon, if you want to change, these are the first steps to doing that. Tell me about yourself? How's your week going? What's going on and let's start from the beginning. Tell me about schadenfreude?' Cosmo has an a A4 pad, writing Ha-yoon's thoughts and feelings down, he opens up about his new relationship with his dad and the positive impact this has had on his life so far. He talks about both his dad and mom meeting on common ground and are trying to move forward with their lives.

Cosmo is acting like a therapist to Ha-yoon, apprehensive at first he eventually sees the positive aspects of doing this and making sense of his feeling and thoughts. 'You might as well get used to this, as there will be multiple sessions of this happening, Ha-yoon. Remember, never listen to someone's advice unless prepared to deal with the consequences.' Cosmo says with a cheeky smile. By changing the dynamics of their working relationship, Cosmo is hoping the Landlord can do more good rather than intimidate people and businesses. He wants him to try to be more constructive with his life and eventually change his schadenfreude mentality.

Over the next few days everything is going well, he has a pre-arranged visit to the Selvante firm. Cosmo wants to see the impact his decision has had in helping them and on the community overall. He is a little paranoid with the whole 'actions have consequences'....thing. At the Selvante meeting he shakes hands with the owners, meets the workers, Sofia and her family. The impact has been really positive much to Cosmo's relief. 'Keep setting the standards, for the rest to follow Leton!' Cosmo thanks Leton the senior lawyer, for working with Selvante and doing his best as role model for other layers at the Rhinemoore Corporation.

Tom always confused as ever, actually admires Cosmo for his down to earth approach, his unique way of solving problems and wanting to help people.

As they are driving back home, Cosmo tells Tom to stop the car, near the park bench, where it all happened. This is where his change of luck occurred, where his fortune changed forever. As he stands in front of the park bench, he smiles to himself. Thinking what were the chances, one in 8 billion roughly or one in one and a half million lawyers in USA that he would be chosen to represent his planet! With an epiphany, Cosmo remembers his first encounter with the Zargboyans and the question he asked himself when he thought he was going to die. How does being a loser make you a winner? He answers to himself, it's because he was a loser they chose him initially, an easy target. All the misfortunes in his past, was it planned? Bad luck? Coincidence? They could have chosen anybody else. But what made him a winner was his resilience to stand up for himself finally and his mental strength to see it through. *I used to have an insular thought process, I don't anymore. Confidence through resilience equals success,* his dad's final life lesson, rings true to Cosmo, as he thanks him in his mind.

'This is where it all started for me, here on the bench, Tom'. Tom confused as ever looks at Cosmo, who then explains, that this was his rock-bottom moment lying on the bench passed out drunk.

'It's gone full circle. If my parents had not experienced their ups and downs in life, I would not be the person I am today.' Cosmo then looks up in the sky and around him, 'Is the whole universe connected in some weird transcendent way? Do things happen for a reason? And either you accept it as your fate, justifying to yourself why your life has turned out the way it has, or do you change your options, re-evaluate your life, take a chance, take a different path which opens up more doors, good or bad? You never know, it could be your greatest adventure yet, who knows, but you won't know for certain, if you never take that first step. I wonder, Tom?'

Tom looks at him in aura, 'Wow, just wow; that is deep Cosmo. I too, have had plenty of rock-bottom moments, deciding do I accept fate or do something about it? Sometimes you can close your eyes, pretend things will go away and everything around you stops. However, the world does not stop, it keeps moving and tomorrow is always a new day of optimism. You have to keep moving, I totally agree Cosmo.'

Cosmo looks at Tom and pats his shoulder, 'You know; I don't know anything about you, Tom apart from you being an ex-Navy SEAL.'

Tom smiles, 'I enjoy working for you, Cosmo, it's definitely been one heck of an experience, I tell you that! I have two beautiful kids, debt ridden and an alcoholic wife in a nutshell.' Cosmo thanks Tom for sharing a snippet of his personal life. 'We will take care of that and help your wife, Tom, let's do some good.'

Back at Hubris Crux, Lucille has been listening to the full conversation via Cosmo's smart phone and tells Tej, 'He has put his foot in it again, more work for me again. Why, oh why primitives are so complicated?' Lucille has her arms up in the air in frustration going around the office. Tej and Alluca both laugh together distracted by Lucille's farzee.

Alluca meanwhile is doing intensive research looking at the biology mechanics of Zargboyan and human species in comparison. She is totally engrossed in her research clutching Cosmo's initial first meeting, piece of paper notes, which still emitting a slight scent of his sweat. She has no idea she is still doing this, whilst conducting her research, using it almost like a comforter.

Eventually Cosmo arrives home, he enters his parents' apartment. As he approaches the front door, it is flung open, he is hugged tightly by both parents and they both start talking at once. Glen has received a letter about getting some private treatment for his lungs, commencing straight away, courtesy of the Rhinemoore Corporation. The whole family rejoice together.

Cosmo eventually makes his way to the bedroom. Both parents decide to ring India to brag about Cosmo's new job and the fact that Glen is now getting treatment. They spend hours over the phone. Jasmine's mom being totally surprised by the news that Cosmo has amounted to anything. In her scepticism, she does a quick search on the internet to find information on the Rhinemoore Corporation, thinking it must be a small local firm. In her research she finds out the sheer scale of Rhinemoore and the new information has been put on the website stating clearly now the head of this firm is none other than her grandson. She sits down to stop herself from fainting, she is astonished. The grandchild who she thought was weak, pampered, weird has come out on top. "Jasmine I think I will come for Christmas after all."

Meanwhile back in Cosmo's bedroom, this good news gives him a boost of courage. He sits on his bed and opens up his laptop, logs onto his bank account but finds it is still showing zero. Over the course of the month he has managed to build on up on his Roobal credits and bonuses especially from the Gauwladyke case. The only problem is; he has no idea how much this converts from Roobal Credits to dollars. Just then, Lucille gives him the go ahead that same night to do the transfer. Cosmo is really excited his first official wage. He activates his business card to do a transfer to his Earth bank account. It takes forever to download and he remembers it's probably because of his primitive 5G network, he places his laptop on the floor and gets into bed ready for sleep and do his nightly vlog.

His balance on the screen laptop eventually says $100 billion dollars' maximum limit has been reached. However, his business card still holds more than three quarters of his earnings. It appears Cosmo has a lot more and a quick calculation would insinuate that Cosmo has roughly just under a trillion dollars' worth of Roobal Credits still waiting to be transferred.

Cosmo contacts Tej to do his regular nightly vlog, an idea that came to him ever since he tried his personal file function on his first day working for the KillaRhinepor Corporation. Every night Tej has been helping Cosmo with vlogging to help him process so much information like a diary or therapy session. This is also one of the reasons why Tej knows so much about Cosmo which puzzles Lucille continuously.

'No doubt FBI will be contacted like Lucille says. I have a dinner with the Zaniyans, we need to help the Munchichi species still. Importantly, Tej how am I supposed to finally get a date with Alluca? In fact, who is Alluca? I know nothing about her. Maybe I need a strategy, Tej, what you reckon? How do I finally tell my parents about my ownership of Rhinemoore and that I'm falling for an alien with three legs and two brains? I think that's a wrap.

Tej, by the way, have you found anything from you past yet?'

Tej can be seen via a hologram from Cosmo's business card, recording these vlogs. 'Miss Alluca, I believe is a complicated individual, Sir, but I think she is the type of person that once she lets you in, you've gained her trust, respect and confidence. Remember it's a privilege not to squander or to dissipate. She has let you in, not the other way around.' Tej speaks in a firm voice.

'I think your right, Tej! For me though, when you had nothing to begin with and truly want something, you will fight for it. Challenge yourself in ways you don't recognise anymore, smashing through the threshold of rejection, what's the worst that can happen? Alluca challenges my anxiety every day, Tej! I raise my game, every day because of her. I wonder if she has two hearts too?' Cosmo says in a curious, passionate manner.

'Very well put, Sir. I can definitely tell you, she has only one heart which is heavily guarded. Your species, Sir, is very intriguing and unique with an enriched history. This, what I think makes your species what it is today. The vibrancy to question, explore, keep searching and loathing for the future and its mysteries, this makes you special. The human species is fascinating with the bonds they make, connecting one and each other by a singular word 'love'; a driving force which surpasses what your species should be capable of. Overachieving the boundaries of expectations, no matter what ideal you focus on, love is the key component here.' Tej then points to Cosmo.

'You are a prime example, Sir. For other species, nostalgia is the driving force that binds them together and motivates them to achieve beyond their limits. For others its pure fear, like the Gauwladykes used to be. For the Jengu species on the other hand, the pursuit of pleasure is the driving force behind their motivations. A question, is Alluca worth the chaos, Sir?' Tej replies with his wisdom outlook on life.

'I always thought as a child my mom's hugs lasted long after she lets me go, especially at the beginning of school. Alluca's the same, in a weird way, her presence, mannerisms, stays with me long after I say goodbye each day, in my mind. Our mind, is the greatest asset I can think of as a species, Tej. Yes, we have cognitive abilities more so on my planet when compared to other animals here. But the mind allows us to plan, imagine, stretch and challenge beyond infinity with no restrictions of what you allow yourself. I think love is a key component of this. In my mind in all the possible scenarios I have created, Alluca is worth the chaos. Could it be even conceivable, mine and Alluca's souls have met before?' Cosmo says optimistically.

'It's certainly possible, Sir, but the odds of that is astronomical and beyond comprehension. To the other point, your species has the ability to create multiple universes in your mind at a whims notice. The potential for that alone is mesmerising. It's the main reason why your species has survived and thrived comparatively, when compared to other dominant species on your planet's history. I also find it really fascinating, no genes, blood, history or tangible connection with Alluca and yet you're willing to risk and take a leap of faith just to be with her in spite of the boundaries that are fore coming. Love is a whole universe unto itself, Sir, one which you should feel blessed to have received when given the chance.' Tej admires Cosmo.

'Maybe I should go beast mode to impress Alluca? I love our nightly chats, Tej, I appreciate it. I never had a brother, sister or someone outside my family to talk to before. How about your past, Tej? Anything of relevance?'

'Oh yes, regarding the on-going search to my history, Sir, I did manage to find out from the Hub City library, old records indicate on Golian 6, that I was somehow picked up from lake 'Galion' all washed up. There was a sticker attached at the back of my head written 'artefact storage,' strange really as that was the reason why I was there in the first place. Such a short amount of time on that planet, it is a bit of a conundrum, even where I was before Golian 6? There are no official records, or it says classified with data being corrupted, a puzzle which I will solve. I will keep searching. Like you, Sir, I never give up.' Tej has a look of optimism about him.

'By the way, this is a beautiful vlog, Sir. I will edit it and store it accurately in my historical records, Sir. Finally, would you like a neck massage, Sir?'

'Go away Tej. Night, night.' says Cosmo, whilst rolling his eyes and falling asleep smiling.

'You too, have a nice sleep, Sir. See you in the morning.' Tej softly speaks and disappears.

In the middle of that night, Cosmo is in his deep sleep, slobbering on his pillow. He is abruptly awoken again by Alluca. As Cosmo comes around mumbling to himself 'right now? Why?' he stares straight at her, rubbing his eyes in the process. The moon is a casting light through his bedroom window. This time, she is sitting on his bed next to him in silent, she stares at him attentively, her cheeks are blushing diamonds!!!!!!!!!!!!!!!!

THE END or MAYBE??

Tom the chauffeur's music playlist for Cosmo:

1. Luttrell ~ Into Clouds
2. Luttrell ~ Out of Me
3. Panama ~ Always
4. Headrillaz ~ Good is Bad
5. Alaya ~ Omnya
6. Lane 8 ~ Stir Me Up
7. Lane 8 ~ Rise
8. Paul Kalkbrenner ~ Dockyard
9. Braxton ~ When the Sun Goes Down
10. Jerro Featuring Kauf ~ Tunnel Vision
11. Luttrell ~ Lucky Ones
12. Chemical Brothers ~ The Test

Whilst driving to pick up Cosmo, Tom receives a message on his phone, it's his wife from the Clinic. 'All debts and repayments have been fully paid.'

'Cosmo,' Tom smiles to himself, as he continues to listen to Cosmo's tunes. 'It really does help you think!'

The Evolution / Revolution approach (ER's) change mindset principle.

3. DECIDERS	4. DO'ERS
'Knowledge sorted. Now decide what you are going to do with it. Decide on the realistic options available, try networking etc. There will be setbacks, Cosmo don't worry that is life.'	'Pay attention, Cosmo'. I've gone through all the principles. From the setbacks, you now have tacitly built resilience without you even knowing it. Build on your new confidence through resilience to succeed in life & honestly do it.'
1. WISHERS	2. THINKERS
'Listen carefully Cosmo' If you wish, imagine or dream to achieve something in life. Don't get stuck in a rut. Move onto principle 2.'	'Think of a strategy to succeed, to make your wish happen, make lists, develop your pool base of knowledge. There will be setbacks, son.'

'The Evolution approach is changing two out of the four principles. The Revolution approach is changing the complete mindset, using the four principles are you still listening, Cosmo? Stop getting distracted and now focus. Some other awesome theories for you, son:'

1. Growing vegetables helps to train you to care for others. Especially me and your mom when were old.

2. When someone in your family can't cook appreciate and enjoy life. The alternative is pointless.

3. Take a deep breath, son, take that split second and prioritise. What's the worst that can happen?

4. When you find your old clothes again, remember it's an awkward history lesson not to forget.

5. To build character, son, force yourself to get insulted at least once a day.

6. By the time you realised life's truths, time is your real enemy.

7. Don't let facts and logic ruin your emotional needs. Accept it and move on.

8. If you can admire your toes, son, no one can insult you. You've already seen your worst self.

9. Schadenfreude just because, it's an awesome word, but has a horrible meaning.

10. If you pollute your surroundings at least get someone else to sort it out. Accountability is key in life.

11. The more different types of music you listen to, the broader your thinking will be.

12. Son, when you meet the right person, you don't need to be a scientist, you just need to be an expert in chemistry, be yourself and not fake.

13. What comes first, you or the family? You obviously! Because if you can't look after yourself, you are no good to the family.

14. Three things you should hate in life Cosmo, which are: arrogance, incompetence and being scammed in finance. Arrogance is confidence without substance.

Now put the TV on, Cosmo' and let's watch some magic!'

Blurb

Blurb

'Change your mindset, Cosmo. Confidence through Resilience equals Success!!' A down and out lawyer, Cosmo Griffin, is given a once in a life time opportunity. It will forever change his life and could save planet Earth, and help dozens of species he didn't even know existed – until now. The question is, does Cosmo have the ability, courage and confidence to do it?